Spine-Tingling

A Village Library Mystery, Volume 7

Elizabeth Spann Craig

Published by Elizabeth Spann Craig, 2022.

SPINE-TINGLING

First edition. May 24, 2022.

Written by Elizabeth Spann Craig.

Chapter One

I poked my head into Grayson's office, holding up a bag of doughnuts and some coffee. "Knock-knock."

He grinned at me, standing up to take the coffees. "Well, hi there. This is a nice surprise."

"Is it? I figured you might be trying to get stuff done before anyone else showed up at work. But I thought that bringing in doughnuts and coffee might be the tickets to get me in."

"As if you need tickets," said Grayson, giving me a light kiss. "Besides, I've got all day to edit these stories. I don't have all day to see you, though."

I sat across from him at his desk. "It's definitely one of those days. I'll be closing down the library tonight, so it's going to be a late one. Plus, I have some errands to run this morning, so I figured I'd better run by while I could."

I glanced around the newspaper office. "Nice place you have here."

Grayson chuckled. "Well, I don't know about that. I spend so much time here that I think I've lost perspective on the place."

It was the kind of office a word person could appreciate. Grayson had the built-in bookshelves fairly bursting with books on every topic—mostly nonfiction, but also some novels crammed in. He had a whiteboard on the wall with scribbles of ideas for stories. There were a couple of stacks of papers on his modest desk, but they seemed organized by clips and binders and had colorful sticky notes scattered throughout.

"It's a lot more organized than I would have thought," I said, slowly. "I mean, your house is organized of course, but I don't think I've ever seen a photo of an editorial office that didn't look like total chaos."

"I've seen exactly the same pictures you have, and I totally agree. But if I start to get a little messy in here, I feel like I can't even think. Do you know what I'm talking about?"

I did. I wasn't a neat freak by a long shot, but I did need to have a sense of order both at work and at home. "I'm guessing if you didn't have things organized in here, it would take you twice as long to get anything done. You'd always be looking for that ad somebody dropped off or a photo that had been printed."

Grayson nodded. "It would take me three times longer to get anything done. But I do have a little bit of fun in here, too. It's just not clutter."

He pointed to the wall behind us and I chuckled. "Star Wars posters. Nice."

"Sometimes it's nice to just think about something besides work."

"Like saving the galaxy?" I asked with a smile.

"Exactly." He took out a glazed chocolate doughnut from the box and took a bite, closing his eyes briefly. "Oh my gosh, these are good. I haven't had doughnuts in forever."

"Me either. For some reason, they were calling out to me this morning. I just need to learn to ignore them if they start calling too frequently."

Grayson said, "I was just thinking today that it had been a couple of days since I'd exercised. I really need to get on it."

"Maybe we can exercise together tomorrow morning? Unless you can leave now and join me before I head into work."

Grayson reluctantly shook his head. "I better not. I have someone coming in for an interview in a little while."

I raised my eyebrows. "New employee?"

"Different kind of interview—a profile I'm writing for the paper."

"Oh, right. Well, let's do tomorrow morning then. If I work out at night, I'll be all keyed up and won't be able to fall asleep."

Grayson took another bite of his doughnut. "I don't think falling asleep is going to be a problem for me at any point today. Just eating this doughnut is making me feel sleepy."

"It's the carbs," I said with a laugh. "Have some of that coffee I brought to counteract it."

Grayson did, after doctoring it with a lot of cream and sugar. "I like my coffee to taste like hot chocolate." He grinned at me.

His phone started ringing and he groaned. I quickly said, "Let me let you go. We'll talk more later."

He waved as I set out with a couple of doughnuts and my coffee. I did want to exercise and figured it needed to be done after I ate in order to burn off the calories I was about to consume. I ran a couple of quick errands and then headed back over to the park and sat there for a few minutes while I enjoyed my doughnuts and coffee. Then I headed into the park for a fast-paced walk. Although I did a lot of walking around my neighborhood, I especially enjoyed my walks at the park. I was rewarded for the short drive by a beautiful vista of mountains behind a small lake. There were plenty of trails to explore, too, with different skill levels.

After exercising, I headed back home to get ready for work. I greeted Fitz, my orange and white cat, who'd been looking out the window and waiting for me. Well, he was probably waiting *and* looking at the birds congregating on my new bird feeders. I decided it was like kitty TV for Fitz—he'd watch the cardinals, chickadees, and wrens with great interest, his tail twitching as he did. Sometimes he'd make little chirping noises as he looked at them as if telling them how much he'd love to be able to eat them if he could only escape outside and subdue nature.

"Sorry, bud—your excitement today will have to be contained to the library," I said wryly. Fitz doubled as the library cat when he was there. Patrons loved him because he was, in essence, a lap cat. I was sure that he lowered the blood pressure of half the patrons in a day's time. I pulled out his carrier and he immediately bounded into it, looking pleased. I was glad Fitz liked going to the library as much as I did.

When I walked in, the library was bustling. Library storytime had just wrapped up and children and their mothers swarmed the circulation desk to check out picture books. It was a sight that always made me smile. I loved seeing what they'd picked out and how they clutched the books to their chests as if they'd gotten a prize. Which, to me, they definitely had. I spotted some of my favorites when I helped them check out: *The Very Hungry Caterpillar*, *Corduroy*, and *The Snowy Day*. I chatted with a couple of the moms about the books and found that they were their favorites, too.

"It makes reading a story over and over again a little bit easier when it's one of the books I loved as a kid," said one of the moms with a grin.

I spotted my favorite patron, Linus, wearing his customary suit and frowning at a chess board on a table near the periodicals. He was sitting with a new friend of his, an elderly man with a bushy white beard that made him look reminiscent of Santa.

Unfortunately, I *didn't* see volunteer Zelda Smith until she nearly ran over me with a book cart when I was on my way to make sure the computers were running as they should. She gave a sniff. "It's important to pay attention to where you're going."

Zelda was both an excellent volunteer and a rather scary one. She was intensely focused on shelving books and did it both swiftly and accurately. However, she was so single-minded that she tended to snarl whenever patrons came up to ask her questions. She didn't even like them to ask *me* questions because Zelda was convinced that I had more important things to do.

I spotted Greta Bowers coming into the library, set to do her own volunteer shift. I gave her a wave and she gave me a small one back. She noticed that I was speaking with Zelda and I hid a smile as Greta carefully avoided us, heading right over to shelve books from a cart full of them.

Zelda gave another sniff. "Greta isn't much help."

"Well, not everyone can be a powerhouse like you, Zelda. Plus, the library appreciates any help we can get."

Zelda grumbled, "She's very slow. And takes lots of breaks."

"She's a volunteer, after all," I pointed out mildly.

"Idle hands are the devil's workshop."

I raised my eyebrows at this. Not only did Zelda strike me as decidedly impious, but I had the feeling that her feelings of dissatisfaction with Greta somehow went deeper than her irritation over slow shelving.

Zelda trundled off with the cart after her intoned quotation, apparently not wanting to possess the idle hands she just denigrated.

I settled behind the reference desk and did some research for a patron who was trying to figure out which hospitals in the southeast had nursing residency programs. For some reason, it wasn't as easy to figure out as one might think. I finally ended up successfully finding information with the American Association of Colleges of Nursing.

Time passed by quickly between the research and some work on an upcoming library program I was helping sponsor. I was so absorbed in what I was doing that I didn't notice Greta standing directly in front of me until she gave a polite cough.

"Greta," I said quickly. "Sorry. I think I got sucked into some work I was doing. What can I help you with?"

Greta actually did look as if she needed some sort of help. She was standing in front of me and shifting from foot to foot restlessly.

"Is everything okay?" I asked, slowly. I had the feeling there was something very much on Greta's mind but that she wasn't sure how to say it.

Greta was about seventy years old and had recently retired from nursing, herself. She had bright, intelligent blue eyes, which currently looked worried, and blond hair with gray strands that fell in soft ringlets on either side of her head.

She hesitated as if she were trying to find the right words. "What would you do if you saw something strange?"

I was used to getting a lot of rather unusual questions at the library. It was actually one of the fun things about the job—never really knowing what you might hear next. But Greta looked so concerned. I said slowly, "Something strange? Like something you saw when you were out?"

Greta nodded. "I saw something odd the other morning when I was walking the dog. Maybe it was nothing, but it could also have tied in with something else. Would you risk looking silly and go to the police?"

"Absolutely. Burton is very easy to talk to and I'm sure he wouldn't think you were silly. Especially if it's something you're concerned about."

Greta nodded again and said, almost to herself, "I'm not even exactly sure of what I saw."

"He'd be grateful that you were being a good citizen and reporting it."

Greta smiled at me, looking a bit relieved. "Thank you, Ann. That's good to know. I'll speak with him later on today."

As she walked away, I could hear her say softly, "I just don't know if it was a push or a fall."

I didn't have time to speak with her again because suddenly the library became very busy. The next couple of hours I spent fixing the copier, which was on the blink for the millionth time, showing someone how to use the ancient microfiche machine in the research room, and showing someone how to synch their e-reader to get their library materials to show up.

At some point near the end of the craziness, I saw Greta leave the library, giving me a distracted wave as she went.

The rest of the day flew by equally quickly. I hosted a book club for moms of young kids, which was a new thing we were trying. I'd certainly hosted adult book clubs and I'd hosted storytimes for kids when I was substituting for Luna, so I tried to merge the two together. We'd had a survey on the library website asking what kinds of programs patrons might be interested in, and a book club for moms came up several times.

I pulled board books and toys into the community room and scattered some mats and pillows on the floor for the moms, figuring they might want to be on the floor with their kids. I'd picked a fairly short read for our first meeting, *We Have Always Lived in the Castle* by Shirley Jackson.

There were ten moms with kids ranging from an infant to a three-year-old, which I thought was a great start. At the beginning, I said that we all understood if kids cried or fussed or if it took a while to gather thoughts. Surprisingly, though, the kids were mostly just great. They were happy to explore since their mothers were still in the room and they flipped through books and played with toys while we discussed what happened to the Blackwood family.

At the end of it, one of the moms came up to me. "Thanks so much for this. I feel like I haven't used my brain for weeks."

"The book was the perfect length, too," another mom said. "Can you find more like that?"

"I've got a whole list of them," I said with a smile. "Thanks so much for coming."

I cleaned up the community room and then headed over to the circulation desk before the onslaught of moms and kids with their book selections arrived.

A few hours later, Luna came over to see me. Usually, there was just one of us closing up each night, but the youth and children's section had been so busy lately, Luna had been working longer hours in the evening.

"How did your new book club go today?" she asked curiously.

Because I knew Luna, I could tell that she was totally wiped out from a very long day at the library. But anyone who didn't know her well would never be able to tell—she still radiated energy. And her eclectic clothing choices, with wildly mismatched vibrant colors contrasting with her currently green hair, served to broadcast it.

"It went really well. I wasn't sure at first if the meeting was going to totally go off the rails or not . . . you just never know when little kids are involved. But it genuinely seemed like a real break for the moms—a chance to be with other grownups and talk about a book for a change. The kids seemed entertained by the toys and books. Plus, I got some good feedback."

"Oh, that couldn't have gone any better. I was thinking about your club last night when I was trying to fall asleep. I have a new idea I want to pitch to Wilson."

I knew she was likely reticent about bringing up her program ideas to Wilson. Not only was he our director, but he was also dating Luna's mom, Mona. Plus, he had something of a history of turning down Luna's ideas.

"What is it?" I asked, giving Luna an encouraging look.

She beamed at me. "Yoga and book discussions for teens. I keep reading about all the stress that teens are under these days. A little yoga might help."

The idea definitely had merit. Plus, it didn't sound like the kind of thing Wilson would turn down. "That's a great idea, Luna."

She brightened. "Think so? As a bonus, it will also help me out by allowing me to wear yoga pants to work."

I laughed at that. "I can't wait to see your yoga outfit." All the yoga pants I'd seen were dark colors. Luna was going to have to really search to find something in hot pink or electric blue.

"You'll love it. Anyway, I guess I'll visit Wilson's office before he leaves for the day and see what kind of mood he's in. You have quite a good track record for getting your programs on the calendar. What's your secret?"

I shrugged. "Nothing amazing. I just write up a proposal and email it over."

Luna gawped at me. "Really? No verbal pitch? You don't go over and present it?"

I considered this. "No, I don't think I've ever done that. Maybe once I've mentioned an idea I had for a program but didn't fully outline it until I emailed it over."

"Do you mind letting me take a look at what you've done? I'm not sure I know exactly what a proposal looks like."

So I pulled up the files from the last couple of programs, printed them off, and handed them over to her.

Luna scanned one of them and made a face. "You have data on here."

"Not *major* data. Just information from other libraries about the kind of engagement they received with similar programs. Wilson is kind of nerdy that way and eats up data."

"Yeah, I guess you're right. You're *definitely* right about Wilson's nerdiness, anyway. I'll revisit it after I come up with some more information. And data." She made the face again.

"It won't take as much time as you're thinking. Plus, as a bonus, sometimes when I'm looking for information on program data, I find ideas for other programs in the future."

Luna brightened. "Good to hear there might be an upside to it all. I could use an upside right now."

I frowned. "Is everything okay? Your mom is doing all right?"

"Oh, she's doing fine. She and Wilson are spending a lot of time together, which makes her happy . . . which makes *me* happy. I think she wishes Wilson were a bit warmer and cuddlier, but you know—Wilson. Anyway, they're doing fine."

"And everything is going all right with you and Burton?"

Luna sighed. "What can I say? He's a great guy. Everyone looks up to Burton. He's solid, funny, and smart. But we're very different people, you know. He's Mr. Law and Order and I'm Miss Zany."

"Opposites can attract, I guess." Although the way Luna was talking, it didn't seem as though she was finding their differences particularly rewarding.

"Yeah, but they also say that birds of a feather flock together." Luna blew out a big sigh. "Sorry. I'm not trying to be such a downer. I haven't even wanted to tell my mom about this because she loves Burton so much."

"But your mom isn't the one dating him," I said.

"Exactly. I keep thinking that Burton deserves better than me."

I frowned. "Now you're being down on yourself."

"No, no. You know I have outrageously healthy self-esteem. I mean that Burton deserves someone who cares about him just as much as he cares about her. I mean, I love going out and doing things with Burton—we have fun going to see movies or going out to eat. But I don't like feeling like I'm being halfhearted or going through the motions with him. Like I said, he deserves better than that."

I was about to respond when suddenly Luna murmured, "His ears must have been burning."

I turned to see Burton walking through the door. He was a heavyset man with kind eyes that often twinkled with humor. He looked serious now, though, as he walked over to us.

"Gosh, he looks grim. I hope he didn't overhear me," said Luna in a whisper.

I shook my head. "There's no way he could have."

When Burton joined them, Luna slid her hand into his and gave it a squeeze. "Everything okay? You look pretty serious."

It was obvious to me that Luna did care for Burton—although it might resemble more of a friendship type of caring. Burton gave Luna's hand a squeeze and a quick, distracted kiss on the cheek. "Actually, I'm at the library for business."

"Needing to head back in the research room again to look up some records?" asked Luna.

He shook his head. "I was wondering more about a woman who might be a volunteer here."

Luna's eyes opened big. "Something happened to Zelda?"

I stifled a sigh. We would get information a lot faster if Burton could get words out.

Burton patiently shook his head. "I wanted to ask about Greta. A neighbor mentioned that she volunteered here."

Luna's eyes somehow managed to open even larger. "Past tense? She's dead?"

Chapter Two

I found myself in the role of being a stereotypical librarian and shushing Luna. The library was a lively place and librarians didn't hush people anymore, but Luna decidedly needed it. There were a few patrons who'd glanced in our direction.

Burton said in a gentle voice, "I'm afraid she is."

I said, "She was volunteering today, actually."

"Did either of you speak with her?" asked Burton.

I nodded. "Just briefly."

"What was her demeanor like?"

I sighed. "She definitely wasn't herself. She seemed very distracted when she came in. As a matter of fact, she was planning on speaking with you today, Burton."

Burton's brow wrinkled. "Did she say what was wrong?"

"Not really." I paused, trying to make sure I got it all right. "She apparently saw something she wasn't sure about. She asked me what I would do in her shoes. I told her that you would appreciate her stepping forward and being a good citizen, regardless of whether she'd been right about what she'd seen."

"But she didn't tell you what she'd seen."

I shook my head. "But she said something when she was walking away. *I just don't know if it was a push or a fall.*"

Burton's eyes narrowed. "That's what she said?"

I nodded. "Sorry, I know that's not very helpful. I thought I'd ask her more questions, but the library became busy."

"Actually, it *is* really helpful. I think she must have been talking about Esther," said Burton slowly.

"Esther Jenkins?" Luna and I chorused.

Burton raised his eyebrows. "You both know her? Was she a regular in the library?"

"Sure," said Luna. "She came through here a lot. You mean *Esther* is dead, too?"

The horrified expression on Luna's face made it look as though she thought people were dropping like flies around her.

"I'm afraid so." Burton reached out and gave her hand a squeeze. "Sorry, I wouldn't have mentioned it in such an offhanded way if I was aware you two had known her as well as you did."

I glanced over at Luna. "I wouldn't say we knew her well, but we always spoke to her. And, of course, she was a fixture downtown. She was often sitting in the square, and I'd pass her on my way to grab lunch if I was eating out. So you're saying she was pushed?"

Burton held his hands up. "I'm not saying anything like that. But apparently *Greta* thought so. As far as the police were concerned, foul play wasn't suspected. She was an elderly woman who didn't have the best balance and was in poor health. She was found at the bottom of the concrete stairs near the fountain in the square."

Luna blew out her breath. "Where the concrete benches are near that little fountain. Was she there a long time? I bet it would have been hard to see her if she was on the ground."

Burton nodded, looking cautiously at Luna as if not wanting to upset her in any way. "The medical examiner thought it had been a little while, yes."

"How did Greta die?" I asked slowly.

Burton sighed. "She fell, as well. Or, rather, was pushed. This time it did look like foul play. She'd hit her head on her granite countertop. Her neighbor found her—the neighbor was supposed to drop by and bring some tomatoes or some such. When Greta's door was open, she walked right in."

"That must have been an awful shock for the neighbor," said Luna soberly. "This just stinks. Greta was awesome and the patrons liked her, too. She was always doing things like sprucing up the library by bringing in more houseplants."

"Did Greta talk with you at all about the incident?" Burton asked Luna.

"She didn't even bring it up. I did speak with Greta today, but I was just blabbing about some new books I thought she might like."

I felt a little sick to my stomach about the whole thing. That must have been evident on my face because Luna quickly asked, "Hey, you're not going to be sick, are you? You all right?"

I reached over and grabbed my water bottle and took a few sips. "I'm fine. I just feel awful about the whole thing."

"You couldn't have known what was going to happen," said Luna pragmatically.

"I know. But I knew she was worried by whatever she'd seen. I wish I'd gotten Greta to call Burton right away."

Luna kept giving me a concerned look and I took another sip of water and leaned back against the front of the circulation desk. She said to Burton, "How are you going to go about looking for suspects? It all sounds really tricky. Are you thinking Greta was murdered because of what she saw? Or do you think she was targeted for some other reason?"

"For now, we're going to try to figure out who might have wanted to kill Esther and try to understand what Greta saw. It seems likely that whatever Greta saw made her a real danger to someone. If we know why Esther died, we might have a lead for Greta's death."

I said slowly, "I can't imagine someone would kill Esther for any reason. She seemed completely harmless."

Burton said, "And she was, for the most part. But think about it—she was always there in the background, always looking, always listening. And she was definitely very sharp, the times I spoke with her. She could well have witnessed something she shouldn't have."

Luna breathed, "Then someone decided to keep her from telling anyone."

Burton glanced at his watch. "Thanks for the info, you two. I'd better head out—the state police are on the way and I'll need to speak with them." He looked at me. "Ann, I know you sometimes have some luck speaking with folks unofficially."

Luna said wryly, "Librarians tend to fly under the radar."

"They sure seem to. But what you both need to realize is that we're dealing with someone who's very dangerous. From what we understand, they've killed twice now. I'm sure they won't hesitate to kill again."

Burton left with a sober wave.

Luna sighed. "Well, that was cheerful. I just can't believe this. Greta? I mean, everybody likes Greta."

I gave a short laugh. "Well, maybe not Zelda. She was saying that Greta was super-slow with shelving books."

Luna rolled her eyes. "Oh, everything is a competition to Zelda. She thinks people are slacking off if they're not charging full speed ahead." She made a face. "Speaking of slacking off, I should head back over to the children's area before Wilson starts wondering where I am."

The rest of the day seemed to pass quickly. The library was still busy by the time I made the closing announcement over the intercom. I made a sweep of the library after everyone had allegedly left and found one old fellow snoring lustily in the periodicals section. I shooed him out gently and then set about putting books on the shelving cart, putting furniture back where it belonged, and generally getting things looking more in order for the next day.

Fitz gave me a questioning look, knowing it must finally be time to head back home. I put the cat carrier on the floor and he happily walked into it, knowing I had a cat treat waiting in there for him.

When we got back to the house, I was getting ready for bed when Grayson called. "Hey there," he said in a soft voice.

I smiled. "Hey there."

"Sorry for calling so late—I know you've got to be about ready to crash after such a long day. I was just wondering if you'd like to meet me for coffee tomorrow morning at Keep Grounded. My treat."

My smile grew. "Sure. I'd love it." I was fond enough of my own coffee, but the coffee at Keep Grounded was definitely a step up.

"Great," said Grayson, sounding as if he meant it. "Sweet dreams."

And in a short period of time, I was having them.

The next morning the alarm woke me up with a start. I grimaced. I usually woke up just slightly before my alarm, which was a much more-peaceful start to the day. I'd been sleeping very hard, though, when it went off. I dragged myself up and headed sluggishly to the shower. Fitz happily curled up on the warm spot where I'd vacated the bed.

Getting dressed, I automatically pulled out my usual "uniform" (as Luna called it) of black slacks and a neutral top. Then I thought about the fact that I might want to look slightly cuter while going to coffee with Grayson. I had this habit of going for the same outfits every day, but I did have some livelier options that were still appropriate for work. Luna might not call them lively at all, but they were to me: black slacks and a pretty rose-colored top. I hesitated and then pulled on some costume jewelry Luna had persuaded me to buy at a thrift store. I looked at myself critically in the mirror. Feeling like it was good enough, I grabbed my purse and headed out the door.

The coffee shop was a cheerful place. There was jazz music playing in the background, lots of light despite the early hour, and brightly painted wooden chairs and tables scattered around the room.

Grayson was already there at a table, typing on his phone. When I opened the door, his face brightened, which made me smile.

He stood up and pulled a chair out for me. "You look beautiful today," he said. Then he corrected himself. "I mean, you *always* look beautiful but you're especially pretty today."

I grinned at him. "Thanks."

"I was going to place an order for both of us. Do you know what you want?"

"Just a regular large coffee. If they could leave room for cream and sugar, that would be great."

Grayson headed over to stand in the very long line. Fortunately, there were a couple of employees working this morning and the owner, Rufus Mitchell, had hopped in to help, as well. I gave Tara Fuller, a friend of mine who worked at the shop, a quick wave and she grinned at me. The smell of freshly ground coffee permeated the air and I felt myself both relaxing and waking up, all at the same time.

A few minutes later, Grayson joined me at the table after doctoring my coffee just the way I liked it.

"How are things at the newspaper?" I asked, thinking about yesterday's revelation about both Esther and Greta. I wasn't totally sure that Burton wanted the suspicious deaths to be public, especially to a member of the press. I was hoping Grayson knew something about it already.

"Oh, they're plugging along. I've been trying to get ahead with my profiles of different townspeople just in case I have a bigger story that I need to follow." He paused. "And it looks as though there might be one."

I gave a sigh of relief. "Good. I was hoping you knew about that already. I didn't want to be the one to spill the beans."

He looked curiously at me. "How did you find out? I mean, other than the fact it's a tiny town and everyone knows everything."

"Burton came over to the library to talk about it," I said quietly. "Greta was a library volunteer."

"Got it. That must have been awful for you to learn about."

I nodded. "She was a nice lady and I'll miss seeing her over at the library. But what really made me feel bad last night was that I'd seen her yesterday before she died. Greta seemed very preoccupied and asked me what I'd do if I'd seen something that might be criminal."

Grayson's eyes opened wide and I hurriedly amended, "Well, she didn't say it in those exact terms. But basically, she'd seen something that worried her. She wasn't sure if it was legitimate or not. I told her that Burton was a great listener and would appreciate her being a good citizen and bringing the incident up to him. I think she planned on talking to him, but she never got the chance."

Grayson said firmly, "That wasn't your fault, Ann. The only person who's at fault is the murderer."

"I know. I mean, of course I know that." The fact of the matter was that I knew it intellectually speaking, but I didn't really *believe* that. I still felt as if there was something I should have or could have done to alter things so they had a better outcome. I continued, "I just think I should have had her call Burton right then. Or maybe I should have called him and handed the phone over to her."

Grayson raised an eyebrow. "So you'd have forced an older lady to talk to the police, when clearly she wasn't sure she wanted to. It sounds like she wanted to come up with exactly what she wanted to say when she spoke with Burton."

"Well, I could have helped her with suggestions for that."

Grayson shook his head. "Ann, you need to absolve yourself of responsibility for this. There's nothing you could have done that wouldn't have been overstepping. It's not as if Greta was your mom or a close friend. She was a volunteer at your workplace. She asked you for advice and you gave her good advice. End of story."

He was right and I finally accepted that. I felt my shoulders release some of the tension in them.

The coffee shop went from being completely full to completely quiet in just ten minutes. I loved the place when it was quiet and happily took a sip of my coffee. Rufus Mitchell, the owner, came over to say hi. He was a handsome man in his early forties with dark hair, brown eyes, and a restless vibe. I don't think I'd ever seen Rufus idle. He was the kind of guy who'd find something to do when things got quiet. He was always updating the coffeehouse, doing much of the work himself.

"How is everything going? Library and newspaper going okay?" He gave us a smile and I could see a little glint of curiosity in his eyes at the fact Grayson and I were having coffee together.

We nodded and Rufus said, "Do you mind if I have a seat for a second? I've been on my feet all morning and they could use a break for a second."

"Sure." Grayson motioned to a chair. "I was going to ask you anyway if you might be interested in being interviewed for the paper."

Rufus raised his eyebrows as he sat down. "That sounds scary. What did I do?"

"Oh, it's nothing bad. We're profiling different individuals in Whitby for a series the paper is running. I think you'll be an interesting person to interview. After all, you probably see most of the folks in town here at some time or another."

He grinned at us. "Probably. People need their caffeine fix. Yeah, okay, I'd love to do it. Just give me a call and I'll check my calendar."

"Great!"

The bell on the door rang then and Burton came in. Instead of heading over to the counter to get a coffee, though, he came over to our table.

"Hey there, Rufus. I was wondering if I could talk to you for a minute."

Rufus gestured to the free chair next to us. "Sure, man. Have a seat."

Burton hesitated. "It might be better to have the conversation in private."

"I don't have any secrets. You can ask whatever you need to in front of Ann and Grayson."

Burton gave a small shrug and sat down in the offered chair. Keeping his voice low and respectful, he said, "I've just spoken with someone regarding the deaths of Esther Jenkins and Greta Bowers."

Rufus looked confused.

Burton continued, "A witness gave a description of a man who was seen roughing up Esther Jenkins. The description matched yours."

Chapter Three

Rufus's eyes grew huge and he glanced quickly around the coffeehouse to ensure no one else was overhearing the conversation. I had the feeling he was starting to regret telling Burton to sit at the table with us.

"What?" he said. "I don't even know who Esther *is*."

Burton's voice sounded a bit stern now. "She's the older woman who spent a good deal of time in the square."

"But I don't know her! Of course I've seen her around. Why on earth would I want to go around bullying old ladies?"

Burton said, "I was informed it was a shove."

"A *shove*?" Rufus gave a short, humorless laugh. "Whoever that witness is must be trying to set me up."

"That witness is dead now," said Burton in a somber voice.

Rufus turned white. "Am I being arrested?"

"Not currently. We're just having a talk. It would help if you could clear up where you were during these deaths."

Burton took out his small notebook and a pen and gave him the dates and times in question. Rufus took his phone out to consult his calendar. "I was working both times," he said with relief, shoving his phone at Burton.

Burton looked at the calendar on Rufus's phone and nodded. "Of course, the coffeehouse does have close proximity to the square. It would be a simple matter to slip out there and then back again. As the owner, I'm sure you can leave the shop whenever you feel like it. I see on the calendar that Tara Fuller was working that morning, too. It's not like the shop wouldn't have had an employee here to cover."

Rufus turned a shade paler than he already was. "I'm not speaking more with you until I have a lawyer."

Burton looked at him thoughtfully for a moment before nodding and closing up his notebook. "Make sure you're accessible in case I need to speak with you again. And, if you think of anything you've forgotten to say about your movements on the days in question, give me a call."

After Burton left, Rufus slumped. He gave Grayson and me an agitated look. "You two know me. You know I could never do something like this. Kill two people? That's what Burton was saying, wasn't it? That whoever killed Esther killed the witness to keep him quiet?"

I noticed that Rufus used the wrong pronoun to refer to Greta. A sign of innocence? Or was he wily enough to do that to divert suspicion from himself?

He didn't seem to expect an answer from Grayson or me because he continued on, almost talking to himself. "I remember the old woman Burton is talking about. I guess she didn't like spending time in her house because she hung out downtown a lot. She wasn't homeless, was she?"

I shook my head. "I think she just enjoyed being outside."

Rufus said, "She'd come into the coffeehouse to sit sometimes whenever the weather was bad out there. She seemed like she took everything in. Maybe she got on somebody's bad side when she listened in to the wrong conversation or something." He looked at both Grayson and me. "Do you know who this witness was?"

We both shook our heads. It wasn't for us to say, after all. Besides, soon it would likely be public knowledge. Better to have someone else tell him.

"Maybe the witness didn't even see what he thought he saw," said Rufus, frowning. "Maybe he was mistaken. Esther was an elderly lady and she seemed pretty unstable to me. She could have just fallen. It could have been a natural death."

"I think the police thought at first that it *was* a natural death," said Grayson.

"Exactly! That's what I'm saying. So why did they decide suddenly that it wasn't? Just because this witness died? But the witness's death could have been natural, too, and just a coincidence." Rufus shrugged. "Even if Esther's death was murder, *I* didn't do it. And I just can't picture anybody in this town murdering a senior citizen. The police must just be looking for something to do."

They were quiet for a moment, reflecting on everything. Then Rufus continued, "Ann, don't you do research work for the library?"

I nodded. "I'm a research librarian."

"Could you help me find a good lawyer in the area? I have the feeling I need to have some decent representation."

"Of course, I can. I'll take a look and let you know."

"Thank you," Rufus said, relieved. "Let me write down my email address for you." He scribbled it on a napkin and handed it over to me. The door opened and several groups of people filed into the coffee shop. Rufus excused himself and hurried over to help them.

I said quietly, "I'm glad he just accepted that we didn't know anything about the witness."

"It seemed like he didn't know anything about it. Unless he's a really good actor. What was your impression?"

"I totally agree. He either knew all about it and rehearsed having an interview with the police, or else it came as a complete surprise to him. I just feel awful about Esther and Greta. They were both such a part of the community—Esther more in the background but still very much a part of the town and Greta more obviously involved, both as a nurse and as a volunteer. It's a real loss for Whitby."

Grayson took a sip of his coffee. "I don't envy Burton trying to figure this out. There are two dead women, both from similar injuries. It does sound like they're connected—like Greta saw Esther being shoved and then the killer had to silence her."

I said, "What I don't understand is why Greta didn't immediately go over to check on Esther if she saw something happen. Esther's body wasn't discovered for some time. Greta was a nurse. It would have been natural for her to run over to see if she could help."

Grayson considered this. "Maybe Greta didn't originally think she *saw* a shove. Maybe she saw Esther falling and thought her killer was trying to grab Esther to help. Greta could have been in a hurry—on her way to something—and the killer could have waved her on. Told her that he was handling it or that Esther was fine. You can't see the bottom of that seating area from the sidewalk, after all."

"And then the killer came back after Greta later to finish her off, realizing she might go to the police once she realized what she saw."

Grayson frowned. "But once she realized Esther died, wouldn't she have *known* what she saw? Understood that she'd seen the murder happen?"

I said, "Maybe she thought Esther was just having balance problems. The square was Esther's usual hangout, anyway. She could have thought she saw someone trying to catch Esther the first time and then Esther had *another* fall later on."

Grayson shook his head. "Like I said, it's a real mess. Burton is going to have his hands full. Now, onto a completely different subject?"

"Please," I said. The current one was rather disturbing to me.

"My friend, Jeremy, has some sort of major project he's having to do for work. He said his house was far too distracting, so I recommended the library."

I chuckled. "Well, the library can *also* be distracting. But not in the same league as someone's home where they're temped to play video games, watch TV, or even clean the house instead of getting work done. I'll keep an eye out for him."

"That's what I hoped." Grayson grinned. "I'm not sure he's set foot in there before so he'll look a little lost and need some direction."

"Got it. I'll be sure to lend him a hand."

We chatted for a few minutes more as we finished up our coffees and then I headed home quickly to pick up Fitz and then head to work. When I walked in, I saw the library was very peaceful. I loved the place when it was bustling, of course and it definitely made the day go faster. But I had a special enjoyment of quiet mornings in the library with the morning light streaming through the old windows. Fitz enjoyed it, too, and quickly found a sunbeam to curl up in as I took my place behind the reference desk.

I worked for a few minutes on a patron request for help with building a resume. After showing him some templates online to format his information and brainstorming ideas for the content, he seemed a lot more confident in his ability to knock it out.

Then I did some work looking for a lawyer for Rufus, since I'd told him I'd help him out with that. I came up with a few possibilities with notes about their education and experience and sent them to his email address.

Before lunchtime, the doors opened to an older lady that I sometimes helped with tech problems.

"Hi, Mrs. Schubert," I said. I noticed she had her laptop with her.

"Good morning, Ann. You must shudder when I appear carrying this device."

I sort of did, but I wasn't about to let her know that. "Of course not. How can I help you today?"

"I have a distant cousin whose mother passed away recently. I've been trying all morning to order a flower arrangement for her from a florist who's local to Columbia, South Carolina. But I can't seem to get online. It's all very maddening."

"That must be really frustrating," I said. "Let's take a look."

I carefully opened her laptop and studied the screen. "It looks like wireless has been disabled," I said.

"Disabled? For heaven's sake. Did *I* do that?"

I knew Mrs. Schubert lived alone, save for a collection of cats. "Sometimes it's easy to accidentally turn things off," I said diplomatically.

"Well, I'll be. Are you able to turn it back on?" The older lady looked quite anxious.

"Absolutely. In fact, I've already done it. Let's connect you to the library wireless and then we can look up florists."

As I was getting her connected, Mrs. Schubert said with a sniff. "Actually, it's no wonder that I'm so scatterbrained. My niece is putting me through the wringer."

"Is she?" I asked vaguely as I pulled up Google to look up florists in Columbia.

"She most certainly is! I give Irene financial assistance and you'd think she could take the time to help me out with computer issues like this. But she can never seem to find a spot on her calendar, despite the fact that she's ordinarily unemployed."

Mrs. Schubert's tone was caustic and I was very glad to be on her good side. I said lightly, "Well, I'm happy to see you and to give you a hand with the problem. That's what I'm here for."

Mrs. Schubert still seemed to want to rant for a while. I knew from experience that when a patron did, they usually felt better afterwards. A librarian isn't *quite* in the same category as a bartender, priest, or hairdresser in terms of hearing people's problems, but it was my contention that we weren't very far behind.

"I'm grateful for your help with this. I wasn't sure what I was going to do and having the task on my to-do list was making me feel quite frantic."

I turned her laptop so that she could see the screen. "I'm delighted to help. Here are the florists that came up in Columbia. Do you have a preference?"

The older woman frowned at the screen. "Who would you choose?"

I said, "Do you know the address for your cousin?"

She nodded and pulled a small piece of paper from her voluminous purse and handed it to me.

I turned the computer back around for a couple of moments and revised the search. "Okay, here are the florists who are closest to that address. That may mean the delivery is not only faster but less expensive. Among these three, this shop seems to be the highest rated."

Mrs. Schubert studied the screen, frowning. "I see. So I'll click on this shop and see what's there."

I gave her a hand with scrolling through the options, clicking on the selection she wanted, and then walked her through the online payment portion.

Once we were done, Mrs. Schubert's shoulders relaxed a bit. "There. I'm so relieved that's over. If you could humor me for one more minute, Ann? I was wondering if you can think of a nonfiction book that might help me deal with my niece. I suppose it would have to be a parenting book, although I'm certainly not Irene's mother and Irene is definitely not a child."

"There are tons of parenting resources out there that should be able to help. Is there a particular area you might be interested in?"

The older lady considered this. "Perhaps something on letting a child make their own mistakes. Allowing them to *learn* from their mistakes. I think I'm bailing out Irene too much—to her detriment. She quits jobs indiscriminately, spends too much money, and then needs cash for the power bill. Of course, she knows in the back of her mind that I'll be there to help her out. Maybe I *shouldn't* be." She paused and then said, "I don't want you to think I'm being stingy with my money. I do have plenty for myself and plenty to share."

"I completely understand. I think you're very smart to consider the problem from other angles."

Mrs. Schubert said, "The problem is that Irene aspires to a grander lifestyle than is realistic. Plus, she's a quitter. She simply doesn't follow through on any of her plans."

She seemed to be waiting on a response from me, so I quickly said, "That must be very frustrating for you."

"It is. It really is. I paid for Irene to have a college education. She was determined to go to a particular school. I didn't find out until much later that she followed a boy there. Anyway, although it was an in-state school, it was a *private* college. I don't have to tell you how much those run."

She didn't. Researching colleges for patrons was a frequent task of mine.

"Well, the college didn't work out for her. The curriculum was too hard, and the boy wasn't apparently who she thought he was. So she ended up dropping out of school. *Completely*. Wouldn't even transfer to a public college or continue her education at a community college. I gnashed my teeth over that one. She's bounced around from waitressing jobs to working at a paint store. She was unemployed until just recently. Now she's a bank teller."

"That sounds like it might be a good position," I said.

"Ordinarily, I might agree with you. But with Irene's lousy work ethic, I doubt there's any prospect for advancement." She sighed. "I shouldn't bother you with all this. Suffice it to say, it's been a real chore to help Irene."

"I have a book I think will help give you some perspective." I looked it up on the computer and then pulled it out of the stacks for her. Mrs. Schubert glanced through it and then checked it out.

"Thank you, Ann. And now I think I might visit with Wilson. Do you know if he's available?"

I knew that Wilson, despite whatever he might be working on, was *always* available for library trustees. And Mrs. Schubert was decidedly on the board. In fact, from what I understood, she was a most influential member.

"I'm sure he is. I'll walk you over there."

Wilson spotted us on the way over and leaped to his feet, opening the door to his office in welcome. "Mrs. Schubert," he said smoothly. "It's so nice to see you today."

I left them together, shutting the door behind me as I walked out.

I'd delved back into writing the library update that was a regular column for Grayson's newspaper when the door opened and Grayson's friend, Jeremy, came in.

I smiled at him, and he looked relieved when he saw me. "Thank goodness you're here," he said with a grin. "I've never been in the library before. It was kind of intimidating coming in here."

The look I gave him must have been completely bamboozled because he laughed. "The expression on your face!"

"I'm just having a tough time imagining the library being an intimidating place," I said, chuckling. "It's always been my second home."

"Yeah, I get that. But I was out in the parking lot watching all the people coming and going. They all look like they know exactly what they're doing: getting books, doing research, whatever. It's hard coming in as a newbie."

I still couldn't picture it, but I tried. "I guess so. Grayson was telling me that you had a big project and were having a rough time working from your house."

Jeremy gave me a rueful grin. "Rough is an understatement. I think part of my problem is the fact that I'm in major procrastination mode."

"So you really *don't* want to work on your project," I said with a chuckle.

"Absolutely not. Working on my project is the very last thing I want to do. So instead, I'm allowing my house to distract me at all times. The dog always needs a walk. The dishwasher always needs emptying. The laundry always needs to be sorted."

"The grass always needs to be cut," said Luna, who'd come up from the children's area. "You're playing my song."

Jeremy gave her a big smile. "A fellow procrastinator?"

"The worst. Ann knows."

I said, "You're not *that* bad, Luna. You always get everything done."

"Sure I do. But I get it done at the very last minute, which is not the way Wilson likes to see things done." She turned to Jeremy again, tilting her head slightly. "We've met before, haven't we? Briefly? At Ann's party?"

I said wryly, "My one and only party?"

"It was a tremendous success," said Jeremy. "Best pre-game party ever."

"Now you're just flattering her," said Luna with a grin. She stuck out her hand, which was beringed on every finger. "I'm Luna."

"Jeremy. I'm a friend of Grayson's," he added. "I'm guessing you've met Grayson."

Luna gave him an impish smile. "Yes, indeed. He's become one of our most loyal patrons, what with Ann over here."

I blushed very faintly, cursing my pale skin. Luna noticed my blush and smirked at me. She said to Jeremy, "Are you pretty new in town? I haven't seen you in here before. Or, at least, I don't think I have."

"You definitely haven't. This is the first time I've made it in here."

Luna laughed. "So I'm guessing desperate times called for desperate measures?"

"Exactly."

I couldn't help but notice the easy manner between the two of them. And the fact that there seemed to be something of a spark.

Jeremy said to Luna, "Maybe you could give me a mini-tour? I feel like I really need to know the ropes before hanging out here."

Luna grinned at him. "That sounds like another procrastination technique. But I'd be delighted to give you the tour. Since you want to put off working, though, I won't give you a *mini*-tour. I'll give you the grand tour."

They set off together, Luna leading the way toward the periodicals section.

I was just taking that in when Burton walked in the library. He glanced around immediately to see if he could spot Luna. His gaze settled right on her and a fleeting sadness crossed his face when he saw Luna laughing at something Jeremy was saying. Then he quickly looked away, giving me a smile of welcome although his eyes looked tired.

Chapter Four

"Hi, Burton," I said. "How is everything going today?"

"Oh, pretty well. We're making some slow progress with the case, but I guess you know that from earlier."

I said, "From the coffeehouse—right. Rufus seemed sort of startled this morning at the news, didn't he?"

Burton said wryly, "I guess it's always a shock to people when they're being questioned in connection with a crime. Anyway, it's a lead we're following." He glanced across at Wilson's office where Mrs. Schubert was still meeting with Wilson. "That's Irene Bell's aunt, isn't it?"

I nodded. "Mrs. Schubert. She raised Irene for most of her childhood, I think."

"How well do you know her?" asked Burton.

"Irene? Or Mrs. Schubert?"

"Either of them. Both of them," said Burton.

I said, "I know Irene from around town. We're close to the same age, too, and I knew her when I was in school. Enough to engage in small talk with, anyway. I know her aunt a lot better since she's a frequent visitor to the library. Mrs. Schubert also sits on the library board of trustees."

Burton raised his eyebrows. "That explains the rapt expression on Wilson's face." He paused. "Have you known Irene to have . . . well, issues?"

I considered this. "Her aunt just outlined quite a few issues with Irene, but I don't personally know of any. Irene is always cheerful and friendly when I've spoken with her. What kind of issues are you talking about?"

"Theft. Problems with the law."

"Wow. No, I wasn't aware of that. Like shoplifting or breaking and entering kinds of things?" I couldn't really picture Irene doing either of them.

"Shoplifting. A clerk caught her doing it some time ago. I let her off with a warning at the time, thinking she'd never do it again. I figured maybe she'd fallen on some temporary hard times because she said she was between jobs."

I nodded. "I got the impression from Mrs. Schubert that being in-between jobs was something of a common occurrence."

"What else did Mrs. Schubert say? She shouldn't be aware of the shoplifting unless Irene told her about it. Even the shop clerk didn't know."

I said slowly, "She didn't mention anything about theft. But she talked at length about the fact that she thought she was bailing out Irene too much. She was unhappy because she thought Irene was wasting her money—at least, that's how I interpreted what she said."

There was another peal of laughter from where Luna and Jeremy, now out of sight, stood. Burton flinched a little and quickly asked, "Wasting her money how? Is she blowing it on expensive items?"

"I think so. But she seemed more troubled by the pattern she saw. She paid for Irene's private college and Irene left school. Irene seems to leave jobs regularly, too, and then Mrs. Schubert helps her out."

"I see."

There was a pause while Burton pulled out a small notebook and jotted down some notes. I said, "Is Irene's shoplifting somehow involved in Esther's or Greta's deaths?"

"I don't really know yet," said Burton in a tired voice. "But one of Esther's friends said Esther mentioned spotting someone shoplifting. Again. I reviewed the camera at the store, which took forever since it's not a very sophisticated surveillance system. Sure enough, it was Irene again."

"So Esther could have seen Irene take something. Irene knew that if you were aware she was involved with shoplifting again, you likely wouldn't let her off with a warning this time. So—she made sure Esther wouldn't say anything. But then Greta witnessed Irene pushing Esther and needed to eliminate her, too."

Burton nodded. "It could have happened that way. It's just one of the angles we're investigating. I'm guessing Irene's aunt wouldn't have been too pleased to find out Irene was swiping things from the local stores."

"Do you think Irene needed money *that* badly? It sounds like Mrs. Schubert has been pretty generous with her."

Burton shrugged. "Not sure. It could be need, it could be habit. It could be that it's some sort of compulsion of hers. Whatever the case, it's concerning. Be careful out there, Ann. I know I've already said that, but I really mean it. I know you can be a magnet for information, but this is a really dangerous individual, whoever he or she is. I don't think they'll hesitate to kill again to cover up their crimes."

He glanced again toward the periodicals section and said, "I better run. Thanks for the information."

And he quietly slipped away as the sound of laughter pealed from the distance.

I wasn't sure what to say to Luna about Burton, if anything. Although Luna and Jeremy seemed to hit it off, it wasn't as if Burton had caught Luna doing anything inappropriate. For all I knew, it could be a blossoming friendship between Luna and Jeremy and nothing more. Somehow, though, I felt like it *was* something more.

The rest of the afternoon passed quickly and soon it was time for me to head out. I packed up Fitz and dropped him by the house, giving him some cat food and a little love.

My phone rang after a few minutes and I smiled when I saw it was Grayson. "How did your day go?" he asked.

"It was mostly okay, I guess." I paused. "Jeremy came by the library today."

"Did he?" Grayson chuckled. "Did he look like a deer in the headlights?"

"At first he did. But then Luna gave him a tour of the library and he seemed to settle in. It looked like he was getting a lot done when I saw him an hour later."

"That's good."

I was quiet again and Grayson said, "Did something else happen?"

"Well, I'm not sure. I might be imagining things, but then Burton got the same impression." I stopped and gave a quick laugh. "Sorry, I'm not making a lot of sense. It's just that Jeremy and Luna seemed to really hit it off."

"Hit it off? You mean as friends?"

"I think I mean that they hit it off as something *more* than friends."

"Uh-oh," said Grayson. Now he was quiet for a moment, too. He finally said, "And Burton noticed that?"

"He did. Luna didn't realize he'd come into the library. You'd think Luna and Jeremy had known each other for years. They seemed really natural with each other. Plus, Luna had just been telling me that she wasn't really connecting with Burton . . . my words, not hers."

Grayson said, "But Luna and Burton always seem to get along so well."

"Oh, they *do*. But Luna thinks of Burton as more of a friend. She likes spending time with him and she respects him, but she said that they're just really different from each other. Of course, Jeremy and Luna seem really different from each other to me."

Grayson considered this. "In some ways, maybe. But they both have the same sense of humor. And I can see Jeremy being attracted to Luna's 'free spirit' vibe."

I sighed. "I mean, there's no reason why Burton and Luna should stay together if they're not suited. It's not as if they're married or anything. I just feel bad for Burton."

"Me too. He's a good guy. But he's also too good of a guy to be dating someone who doesn't feel the same way he does. He needs to be in a relationship where the woman is just as crazy about him as he is about her."

I said, "That's pretty much what Luna said. She and I were talking about Burton before Jeremy even came in. She was saying the relationship was lopsided and she felt bad for Burton."

"It'll work out for the best, Ann. And who knows . . . maybe Jeremy and Luna *will* end up just being friends."

"Maybe," I said. But I had the feeling that wasn't going to be the case.

"On a completely different subject—would you be at all interested in heading over with me tomorrow to see Freddie Jenkins?"

"Esther's son? Sure. Why are you meeting up with him?"

"I told him that the newspaper would like to do a story about his mother. Although not everyone knew Esther, most people recognized her. She was a real fixture downtown, after all."

"Sounds like a great idea."

"Great. Freddie said tomorrow morning, pretty early, would work out better for him. What's your schedule like tomorrow?"

"I don't have to be at the library until after lunch, so that's perfect. See you then."

The next morning, I woke up and put on my usual work clothes since I wasn't sure how long I'd have to change before going to the library after lunch. I was unusually hungry, so I made myself a big breakfast of scrambled eggs with spinach and a bowl of cheese grits.

Grayson came right on time. "I brought some coffees for us. Cream and sugar?" He handed a travel mug to me as I climbed in his car and I gave him an appreciative smile.

A few minutes later, Grayson pulled the car up to Esther's old house. We could tell that Freddie had definitely been doing some work there. There were boxes stacked high with items from the house and a bag of what appeared to be clothes in the yard, too.

The house was a small brick home that looked as if it could use a few repairs. The roof was in pretty poor condition, as was the trim. The yard itself was mostly red clay with some tree roots poking through. I figured it was no wonder why Esther didn't spend much time here.

Freddie emerged from the house lugging another box, which he unceremoniously dumped in the yard. He had the same wild, frizzy hair that his mother had, along with her bright blue eyes. Like hers, his eyes seemed to take everything in.

Grayson gave him a wave and said quietly to me, "Do you know Freddie at all?"

"Barely. Once, when his air conditioning was broken, he spent a whole two weeks at the library until Esther reluctantly paid for his air to be fixed." I paused and said, "That's all according to Freddie, anyway. He's quite the talker. He's also been in and out of the library while he's been job hunting. I've helped him out with his resume, too."

Freddie brushed himself off as if he was covered with dust and walked over to greet them as they got out of the car. He grinned at me and said, "Don't spend all your time at the library, then? I sorta thought you lived there."

Looking at him, his features were so similar to his mother's that it was almost eerie looking at him.

"Sometimes I feel that way," I said with a smile.

"And the cat? Does he stay there overnight?" asked Freddie.

"No, Fitz comes home with me in the evenings."

Grayson said, "I hope it's okay if I brought Ann along for the interview, Freddie."

"Of course it is. She's probably interested in this stuff." He paused. "I guess I can invite you in but we might have to be creative with where we sit. I've been clearing everything out."

"Getting ready to sell the house?" asked Grayson.

"Nope. I figure I can live here. I just have to get it to the point where I can put my stuff in. Mama had a bunch of junk here."

We walked inside the dimly-lit house and I realized creativity with seating was definitely going to be required. I chose the top of a rickety-looking cedar chest. Grayson balanced delicately on the top of a spindly stool that made him sit quite taller than Freddie and me. Freddie, perhaps knowing the unreliability of the rest of the furniture, chose to sit on the floor with his back against the wall.

"Doesn't look like much here, does it?" asked Freddie. "You'd never guess Mama was rolling in it." He looked at Grayson. "You can print that in the paper if you want. I know how people looked at Mama. I figure they thought she was homeless or something. She never spent much of anything on herself, but she believed in putting money in savings. Now I've got that money coming to me." He frowned. "Only problem is the cops think I might have done my mother in for the money. That's why I want you to print where I was when she died. I don't want the whole town thinking I've done her in."

Grayson pulled out his phone and said, "Is it okay if I record the interview? It helps me keep everything straight."

Freddie nodded impatiently; the details of the interview not important to him. "Anyway, I was in Quittin' Time drinking with my buddies when Mama died. At least, when the cops *say* that Mama died. I don't guess anybody really knows when that was, exactly. I didn't have anything to do with it. Make sure you put that in there."

Grayson nodded. "Of course I will."

Grayson was excellent at what he did. I knew that his features usually didn't include relatives denying they murdered the local in question. But I had no doubt he'd be able to finesse it somehow.

Grayson said, "Has your situation already improved or are you having to wait for the estate to go through probate?"

Freddie said cheerfully, "Things are definitely better already. I joined my mom's account a couple of years ago when she needed some help managing her bills. Now the money in that account doesn't have to go through probate. The house is a different story." He looked glum.

"If you're planning on moving in the house, though, I guess that doesn't matter," I said.

"Right you are, Ann! Now I don't have to pay rent anymore. It's working out great." Maybe he realized he sounded a bit too gleeful because he quickly wagged a finger at us. "Don't think I was taking advantage of my mom, either." He looked over at Grayson. "Maybe you should add that to your story so people won't get the wrong idea. I was *helping* my mom out. And, believe me, she kept an eagle eye on the books. I didn't even buy a stick of gum from her checking account unless I asked her first."

Grayson said, "It sounds like your mom was a sharp lady. Can you tell me more about her? Where she grew up, for instance?"

For the next fifteen minutes, Freddie regaled us with tales of his mother. It did seem he had a deep fondness for her, despite his avaricious delight at suddenly coming into her money. Esther had grown up in Tennessee, had married young, followed her husband to Whitby and settled down. Her husband had died in a car accident, leaving a hefty insurance policy which she never touched. She'd also been rather frugal.

I asked, "Did she work outside the home?"

Freddie stuck his chest out a little. "Now *this* is something you're going to want to stick in that paper of yours. Mama was an inventor."

"Was she?" Grayson looked startled and I must have too because Freddie grinned at both of us, showing off various fillings.

"You don't believe me, do you? Maybe you think Mama was sort of slow just because she liked spending time sitting outside and observing people. But she wasn't. Nope. I can't tell you much about her invention because I never did really understand what she was talking about. Never cared to, either. But whatever she invented helped planes to run better somehow."

We stared at him. "That's amazing," I finally offered.

Freddie shrugged. "Mama used to be an engineer but quit when she made all that money from selling her invention. Decided to spend her time sitting around outside."

"Maybe she was still coming up with other ideas," said Grayson. "She could have been seeing blueprints in her mind while she was outside."

Freddie gave a laugh. "Maybe. That's not for me to say. All I know is that she liked being outdoors."

"How was your relationship with your mother?" asked Grayson. "Did you have much in common?"

I suspected the answer to this was no. It sounded like Esther had been an extraordinary person—one I was regretting not having known better. Freddie didn't seem exactly the same caliber, at least intellectually speaking. I wondered if he'd been anything of a disappointment to Esther or if she really hadn't had any ambitions for her only child.

Freddie said, "Oh, Mama and I got about real well. We were chums. I worried some about her being outside all day but then I saw how much she liked being out of the house. I guess Mama was different, though. There's a word for it." He looked over at me.

"Eccentric?" I asked.

"That's it! That's the one. Mama was sorta eccentric." His face darkened. "I just hate to think that somebody killed her in cold blood. Makes me want to get back at them."

Grayson asked, "Did you mother ever talk about things she'd seen when she was spending those long days outside?"

Freddie considered this. "Nope. Not really." Then his face lit up. "Well, maybe. You want to know what happened to my mom? I bet the neighbors probably know. Because Mama didn't just sit outside downtown—she'd sit out in the yard here, too. She'd pull out a chair and just sit."

"What are the neighbors' names?" asked Grayson.

Freddie screwed up his face in a considering expression. "Let's see. Weird names. Ah. Brownie and Lyle." He made another face that passed judgement on their names.

"Did you speak to the police about them?"

Freddie shrugged. "Nope. Didn't think of it until now."

Freddie was starting to get antsy, so Grayson did a nice job wrapping up the interview by asking more softball questions to help round out the piece.

Then Grayson said, "Mind if I take some pictures to accompany the article?"

Freddie lit up. "Sure. How about me with my new car?"

As Freddie led us back outside to the car, I couldn't help but think that standing with a sporty car wasn't exactly going to convey the image Freddie was hoping to leave with the good folks of Whitby. If he'd wanted to demonstrate that he didn't have a motive in his mother's death, that wasn't the best way of doing it.

Grayson took a few more pictures of the house and grounds and then thanked Freddie for his time. Freddie immediately scurried back into the house to continue his clearing activities.

Chapter Five

I said in a low voice, "Freddie reminds me a lot of Irene Bell. At least, from what I've *heard* about Irene. Do you know her?"

Grayson shook his head. "I don't think I've met her."

"According to her aunt, she's something of a big spender."

Grayson chuckled. "I don't know what it's like to be a big spender. And, if I'd wanted to find out, I should probably have picked a different profession."

"Same," I said dryly.

"I'm going to head next door and talk to Brownie and Lyle. Want to join me?"

I felt a little leery. "The neighbors? You're just going to go knock on their door?"

Grayson shrugged. "They might be able to provide a different perspective on Esther. It wouldn't go in the article, of course, but it might help shed some light on why Esther died. Freddie seemed to think they weren't crazy about Esther and sometimes it can be hard to get that kind of information after someone dies—they end up being automatically treated like saints."

I followed him next door where I was relieved to see a teenager tinkering with an old car in the driveway. We wouldn't have to knock on the door after all, it appeared. The work seemed to be something involving his muffler, which I had the feeling was going to end up making it extremely loud.

Grayson called out in a friendly voice, "Hi there."

The young man warily looked over at him. "Hi." He crawled out from under the car and looked at us suspiciously through long hair that flopped over his face. He was wearing all-black clothing.

Grayson said, "You must be Lyle."

"I haven't done anything," said Lyle sullenly in what I took to be his usual knee-jerk reaction.

"No, of course not. I'm with the newspaper and am doing a story on your former next-door neighbor."

Lyle's expression was scornful. "What, on *her*? What for?"

Grayson decided to answer this with a question of his own. "Did you know her? Esther?"

Lyle snorted. "I didn't *know* her. All I know is that she was a real nosy lady. I'm not sorry she's dead at all. She never minded her own business."

Grayson looked a little taken aback by this declaration. "Got it. So you weren't a fan of hers."

"All I know is that I never do anything to hurt anybody. She just didn't like my music. All she ever did was complain. As soon as I'd drive up, she'd come charging up and yell at me for being loud. It wasn't even *that* loud."

I found that hard to believe. Everything about Lyle screamed "loud."

"Right," said Grayson. "Listen, is your mom or dad at home? I wanted to see if I could get their perspective for the paper."

Lyle snorted again. "My dad is never home," he said in a bitter voice. "Mom is there, though. Just knock on the door."

"No school today?" asked Grayson. "That must be nice."

He gave Grayson a scornful look. "Teacher work day."

The house was one of those deliberately ostentatious houses that appeared to be trying to make a point. The lot the house was sitting on wasn't large, but the house was tremendous. I wondered if a smaller house had been razed to build the stone edifice in front of us.

Grayson rang the doorbell and we could hear Westminster chimes playing. He gave me a wink.

The door opened to reveal a well-dressed middle-aged woman with very blonde hair and an immaculate manicure. "May I help you?" she asked in a rather snippy voice.

Grayson gave her an expansive smile. "Hi. Are you Brownie?"

She nodded, looking about as suspicious as her son had minutes before. "I don't need anything, if you're selling things."

Grayson said in a soothing manner, "We're actually here to get a little background on a story I'm writing about your neighbor."

Brownie looked slightly more interested. "Really? A story on Mildred?"

"No, actually. A profile on your other neighbor—Esther Jenkins."

Brownie looked completely flabbergasted. "Seriously? An article on *her*?" She seemed to consider whether to invite us in or not. Finally, her curiosity won out. "Would you like to come inside?" she asked in a rather reluctant voice.

We followed her into the cavernous foyer and into an equally tremendous living room. It was decidedly not a cozy home. The decorating was minimalistic with a black and white design. It was the kind of place where I'd have worried about eating or drinking for fear I'd spill on something. Fortunately, Brownie made no move to offer us any sort of refreshments. I ended up carefully perching on what I suspected was an Eames chair.

Grayson sat on an equally expensive looking chair, giving Brownie a friendly look the entire time. "Do you decorate for a living? It looks fabulous in here."

Grayson was being nice, and it seemed to be warming Brownie up a little bit. Her shoulders relaxed and she sank gracefully down on a very modern looking sofa that didn't appear in the least bit comfortable to me. "I'm not, but thank you. I'm a social media influencer, actually."

"That must be a very interesting job," said Grayson politely.

Apparently, talking about being a social media influencer was fine with Brownie. "Oh, it's been great. I take my own pictures, but I'm thinking I may need to spring for a photographer soon for some of my shoots. Maybe you have people at the paper who do that kind of thing. Take pictures."

"We do have a photographer on staff."

I smiled a little. Grayson sounded a little wary and I couldn't blame him. He wouldn't want the photographer for the paper being lured away by a social media influencer. And, judging from the house and Brownie's expensive attire, she might be able to offer more money than Grayson could.

Brownie gave a smirking smile. "I'll have to see if he can help me out with some shoots. In his off-hours, of course."

Grayson seemed to want to shift the conversation away from his staff photographer—who was actually a woman, despite Brownie's assumptions. "What kinds of things does your social media focus on?"

"It's lifestyle stuff. So what I'm wearing, where I travel, what I eat. And parenting, of course." Brownie said with a sigh, "You know, it's not easy raising teenagers. Plus, I'm doing it pretty much on my own because my husband travels so much for work. I've done the best I can, under the circumstances. The band practices stopped, for one thing."

Grayson said, "I'm assuming Esther might not have liked the noise? Was that why you stopped them?"

"As if!" said Brownie with a snort. "I didn't care what she thought. She was just looking for something to complain about. No, I stopped them because I didn't like the other boys in the band. I thought they were bad news and didn't want to have them around Lyle."

I had to wonder what Lyle thought about that. I was sure Brownie's heart was probably in the right place but banning friends must have been tough on Lyle. Maybe that's one of the reasons he was so sullen looking.

Grayson said sympathetically, "They were bad influences, you thought?"

"Totally. They always showed up here high on something. That's the last thing we needed over here, you know? Lyle is a great kid, and he can find other friends."

From what I saw outside, I imagined that Brownie didn't include the surly Lyle in too many of her pictures for social media.

Brownie appeared to bore of the topic and asked, "Now what exactly are you writing about Esther?"

"It's a profile. Esther was something of a fixture in downtown Whitby and everyone knew who she was but no one really *knew* her. I'm hoping to correct that."

Brownie didn't seem particularly impressed by this plan. "I'm not sure you're going to find out anything very interesting. Not interesting enough for a story, anyway."

Grayson said carefully, "Your son didn't seem like he was very pleased with Esther. Could she be difficult to deal with sometimes?"

I could see a fierce glint in Brownie's eyes and realized she was a mama bear type. Her entire demeanor indicated that we should leave Lyle out of it. "He's just a boy. Esther should have been more understanding or at least tried to remember what it was like to be a teenager. Being a teen is very hard these days; they have all sorts of social pressures to deal with. Social media is very stressful, you know—everyone is always trying to look perfect all the time."

I thought it was interesting that Brownie would take this particular viewpoint since I had the feeling the life she presented on social media as an influencer was sure to portray her family and life in the best possible light.

Brownie continued listing all the pressures today's youth had to grapple with. "Getting into college is also much harder than it used to be. To get into a good school, students have to take really rigorous classes, *plus* have leadership positions in different school organizations. They have jobs and homework, too. So what I told Esther is if Lyle wanted to let off a little steam by playing his music loud for a few minutes, he should have been able to do it without her complaining about it. Besides, she was pretty deaf—I'm sure it didn't even sound that loud to her."

This made me raise my eyebrows and I couldn't resist putting in my two cents. "Deaf? It sounded like she overheard a lot for her to have been deaf."

Brownie sniffed, giving me an irritated look. "Maybe she had her hearing aids in when she was being nosy. She definitely was a busybody."

Lyle slouched into the house, hearing the last bit. He snorted. "You must be talking about the old lady again."

"Esther, yes," I said, feeling irritated and defensive on Esther's behalf.

Brownie quickly said, "Lyle is feeling annoyed because the police have been asking questions. Just because we live next door, of course, not because we're suspects or anything. Answering questions from the police is a scary thing for children."

Lyle gave his mother a scornful look at the word "children". Then he said, "Like I even know what I was doing when Esther died. One day kind of slides into another around here. I can't wait to graduate and get out of this town. Nothing ever really happens here."

Grayson asked, "Where are you planning on going to school?"

Lyle shrugged. "As far away as possible."

Brownie gave Lyle a quelling glance. "You shouldn't say you don't know where you were when Esther died. You know exactly where you were. It was just a normal day."

"Did you think anything about her death at the time?" asked Grayson. "Did you think it could possibly be suspicious?"

"Of course I didn't. An old lady had a fall—that happens all the time. It was unfortunate but hardly unlikely. I'm not sure where the police are coming from with investigating the whole thing."

Lyle drawled, "I didn't care one way or another what happened to her. All she did was cause trouble. I didn't need that kind of distraction in my life. I've got to focus on my future."

I noticed he said the words in a rote kind of way that suggested he was repeating what his mother had said many times before.

Grayson still managed to give the despicable Lyle a friendly smile and an interested look. "What are you thinking about doing once you've finished school?"

Lyle shrugged again. "Maybe be a surgeon or a lawyer or something."

Brownie beamed at him.

I couldn't resist saying, "You must be doing great at school then."

Lyle gave me a sour look. "Well enough."

I noticed he shifted uncomfortably on his feet, though, and was frowning as if he'd only just realized the correlation between good grades and the two professions he'd casually mentioned.

Brownie said, "I really want him to go on an engineering track like his father. His dad's got all sorts of connections and would be able to get him really set up."

I wondered if Brownie knew that engineering was not all about connections. It also involved school, math, hard work, and certifications.

Brownie seemed to read my mind because she said, "There will be school, of course. But Lyle can handle it. He's good at juggling the different pressures he's under."

Grayson said, "I'm sure he'll do great, no matter what Lyle decides to do."

Brownie gave him a simpering smile. "I'm sure he will, too. Anyway, back to Esther. You've likely gathered that we didn't have the best relationship with her, but it was all because of the way she treated Lyle. It was ridiculous of her to target him like that. I did try to reach out to her and be nice. One day I popped over next door with an apple pie."

"That was nice," said Grayson with a smile.

Lyle snorted, giving his mother a look.

Brownie said, "Wasn't it? Except Esther apparently didn't like apple pies. Who doesn't like apple pies? I found her a deeply unpleasant person and I didn't try to develop any sort of a relationship with her after that."

"Do you have any ideas who might have done something like this to Esther?" I asked.

Lyle shrugged. "Who'd want to kill an old lady?"

Brownie shrugged too, looking almost identical to Lyle. "Unfortunately, I have the feeling Esther wasn't the most popular person in town. Right? I mean, look at our own dealings with her. I wish she'd done something to fix up her property, too. It's really been an eyesore and has probably devalued our own property, considering we're right next door."

I didn't mention that Brownie could have chosen another lot to build on. Esther's house was decidedly there first.

"We were interested in buying the lot from her," said Brownie. "We made a *very* generous offer. I thought we could build a guest cottage on Esther's property for when my mother came to visit. We'd have torn down the house, of course." Brownie's lip curled a little to indicate her feelings about Esther's home. "But Esther wasn't interested in getting rid of it."

Brownie didn't seem to realize she'd given herself a viable motive for wanting Esther dead.

Grayson said, "We just came from the house and it looks like her son is clearing it out nicely."

Brownie nodded. "I've seen him over there before. He looks like the kind of person who lives beyond his means. Maybe Freddie was in a hurry to get the house. You never really know people, do you?"

Grayson said, "You think Freddie could have killed Esther in order to inherit her house?"

Brownie quickly said, "I didn't say that. I just think money is often a big motive for murders." She looked pointedly at her expensive wristwatch. "And now I'm afraid I have things I need to take care of. I'm sorry Lyle and I couldn't be more help."

Lyle gave them that smirking smile again.

Brownie opened the heavy door for us and then paused. "You know, Ann, I did have one question for you." She paused. "Sorry I thought you were selling things when you first came over. I do recognize you from the library now, of course."

I gave her what I hoped was a nice smile.

"I know a couple of people on the library board of trustees. I would love to get closer to one of them and do some networking. I thought perhaps I might get more information on getting on the board."

"Absolutely," I said. "Come by the library any time and we'll be happy to fill you in. It's a pretty simple process. You might also be interested in reading the minutes from the meetings, which are publicly posted on our website." I devoutly hoped that Brownie would read some of the minutes and decide that being on the library board was not for her.

"Thank you. Oh, and I think I'll see you more frequently since Lyle is going to be meeting with a tutor there for math. Math grades are very important for engineering."

Lyle looked even more sour than he had previously.

I said, "There are a lot of students getting tutoring over there. It's a great environment for some extra work on a subject."

Brownie turned to Lyle, "Oh, we'll have to take a selfie at the library. It's the perfect background. I can tag it with all kinds of educational tags."

"No." Lyle didn't even try to cooperate with that particular idea.

Grayson and I both jumped a little as Brownie blew up at her son. "You'll do it and like it, Lyle. I'm getting tired of this attitude."

She continued ranting as Grayson and I quickly took our leave.

"Wow," he said as we got into his car.

"I honestly can't tell which family dynamics I found more disturbing—Freddie and Esther's or Brownie and Lyle's," I said.

"Oh, I think Brownie and Lyle's, hands-down. So, does she dote on Lyle as much as she made it sound? Or is it more that she wants the *appearance* of being a devoted mom but she really is using Lyle as part of her influencer gig?"

I thought about Lyle for a moment. "I think maybe a little of both? She definitely seems protective of him, but is also totally focused on getting the next perfect photo to show her perfect life."

"Which is clearly as imperfect as the rest of ours," noted Grayson dryly. "But I do feel sorry for Lyle."

I tried to summon up the same feeling but fell a little short. Maybe he was better when he wasn't feeling defensive. Or wasn't around his mother.

Grayson continued, "He didn't ask to be put in that position. It seems to me that he's being used almost like a prop for Brownie's social media business. I'd probably have been sullen and unhelpful at his age, too, if I had to deal with that."

"That's very generous of you. Maybe Lyle acts a little better when he's away from home. I'll have to see how he is at the library."

Grayson said, "It almost sounded as if Brownie planned on driving him over there, herself. She mentioned 'seeing you more.' I wondered why she might do that since it's obvious Lyle can drive himself."

"Maybe to make sure he actually goes to math tutoring? Or maybe because she wants to take pictures of the library for her social media?"

Then we chatted about other things for the quick drive back to my house.

"Do you want to come in for a while?" I asked as I climbed out of the car.

"I wish I could. I need to get back to the office and check on things there. I think I got a couple of text messages while we were out."

I asked, "Did you get enough information for your article?"

Grayson said ruefully, "I did, although I think it's going to be a shorter profile than I'd planned. Freddie was the only one who offered any useful information. Maybe I'll try to find some of Esther's friends and see if I can find out more."

I wondered if Esther had many friends since I'd always seen her solo when she was in the square. It made me feel sad and I wished I'd managed to be more outgoing and spoken to her more when I'd had the chance.

Grayson pulled up in front of my house. I said, "I guess I better run some errands before I head inside. Otherwise, I'll end up cuddled up with Fitz on the sofa."

Grayson chuckled. "I didn't think you minded curling up with Fitz on the sofa."

"I love it. But it means I don't get anything done." I hopped out of Grayson's car and into my own. He answered a text message while he was still parked and I started up my car. The ignition didn't go well. My old car made all sorts of awful groaning and grinding noises in response to the key turning.

Chapter Six

I glanced over at Grayson and saw him grimace. He finished up his text and climbed back out of the car. "That didn't sound good," he said.

I found the car's manual in the glove compartment and flipped back to the troubleshooting section while Grayson peered under the hood.

"Any ideas?" we asked each other simultaneously.

Grayson said ruefully, "Unfortunately, I'm pretty useless with cars unless they need oil, have a flat tire, or require a new battery. Or windshield wipers."

"I have the feeling none of those are going to apply in this case." I sighed. I did an online search and winced. "Loud noises might mean problems with engine belts, heat shields on the exhaust, and other dire-sounding things. Should I even drive the car like this?"

"*Can* you drive it like that?" asked Grayson.

"I can give it a go."

I must have sounded reluctant because Grayson quickly said, "How about if you drive it to the garage for a checkup and I follow you to make sure it doesn't break down on the way over?"

We made a very short, slow-moving parade as I headed over to Ted's Garage, now run by Ted's brother. My car complained during the commute but did get there without falling apart along the way.

I waved Grayson on. "Thanks. I'm good now."

"Are you sure? Won't you want a ride back home from the garage? It might take a while for them to fix the car. They might even have to order new parts."

"Oh, they always have a loaner car available. I'll be fine. You head on to work."

Grayson took off and I headed inside the office of the garage. There I saw Zelda, nicely dressed and watching me enter the door through narrowed eyes. Zelda ensured the office was immaculate and protected it like a lion with her cub. When she first started working there, the office had been completely chaotic until Zelda had whipped it into shape. The new owner preferred working under the hood to working in the office, so he was delighted to keep Zelda on. And *I* was delighted that Zelda was kept busy instead of harassing members of the homeowner's association, which was her previous favorite thing to do.

"May I help you?" asked Zelda coolly.

"Hi Zelda. I started up my car a few minutes ago and it made some really horrific noises. I was wondering if someone could take a look at it for me."

There was an accusatory look on Zelda's face as if I'd deliberately sabotaged my own car somehow. She said, "That might take some time."

"Is the shop as backed up as it was?"

Zelda pursed her lips. "I'll have to consult with the mechanics to see what sort of timetable we'll be dealing with." Before I could answer, she bustled away into the garage. She returned just as briskly. "You should be able to pick up your car in the next day."

"Do you have a loaner vehicle I can borrow?"

Zelda shook her henna-red covered head. "Already loaned out."

Now I was feeling a little worried and realized I shouldn't have dismissed Grayson so blithely. Luna was working. Zelda was working. Grayson was working. I decided to see if I could catch Grayson before he headed into a meeting . . . but found I couldn't catch him on the phone.

"You could always wait here for it." Zelda gave a throaty, coughing laugh.

"I've left a message for Grayson. Until he gets it, I might just hang out in the waiting room for a while."

Zelda nodded. "Coffee's over there." She pointed a red-tipped finger at a nearby table. "Snacks are there." She pointed in the opposite direction. "Snacks aren't free—we use the honor system here." She gave me a look as if to say that she strongly suspected I wouldn't follow such a system.

I fervently hoped Grayson would get back to me soon as I settled into a very sanitized-looking chair in the waiting area and watched as Zelda took out cleaning wipes and proceeded to wipe down the equally-sterile-looking counter.

To pass the time, I decided to take a stab at conversation. "I know you knew Greta, Zelda, at least from the library. What do you make of . . . well, everything?"

Zelda gave a sniff. "I wasn't surprised."

"You weren't surprised that Greta ended up *murdered*?" This seemed extreme, even for Zelda.

Zelda gave me an irritated look. "Maybe the police are wrong about the two things being connected. I know all about their thinking because Burton asked me questions since I knew

Greta. Maybe Esther really did just fall down those stairs. She wasn't all that stable on her feet, you know."

I knit my brows. "So you're saying that Greta was always the intended victim of the murderer."

Zelda gave an eloquent shrug. "Could have happened that way."

I looked at her curiously. "Why didn't you like Greta? She always seemed perfectly lovely whenever I saw her."

"Thought she was better than everybody," proclaimed Zelda.

"Did she?" I hadn't gotten that opinion at all. Maybe she'd simply made the mistake of letting Zelda know she'd considered herself better than Zelda.

Zelda apparently thought it was time to dive back into work. She gave a dismissive sniff and pulled out a bunch of invoices.

I decided to kill some time on my phone. But first, I realized I could probably knock out a little work while I was experiencing this dead time. I had photos I'd already taken that were on my phone and could be uploaded online. After I updated the library's social media platforms with pictures of Fitz looking alluring alongside several of our new books, I took an online detour to look up Brownie's Instagram. A pattern quickly established itself as I scrolled through her photos. There were pictures of Brownie looking elegant in various expensive-looking outfits in different rooms of her house, always with the designers mentioned in the posts.

In other photos, she showed perfect, healthy meals that she'd allegedly prepared. I don't know why I felt so doubtful about Brownie's cooking prowess, but I did find it hard to believe that she was spending her day cooking vegan food. I suspected there might be a caterer involved somehow.

There were also pictures of her husband and Lyle. She was clearly able to get Lyle to pose for pictures, at least sometimes. There was always a smile on his face, although I noticed a certain tightness to his features. I couldn't blame him—the last thing I wanted to do when I was his age was have my picture taken. I wasn't wild about it now, either, which was why I was so delighted to have Fitz step up to the plate for the library's social media accounts.

Brownie's husband was mostly absent from the pictures, but when he was part of them, it was always perfectly presented to her followers. His name was apparently Blaze, which made me raise my eyebrows. Blaze did seem to participate whole-heartedly when he was in a post. He was always wearing expensive-looking casual clothing—a white shirt with an open collar that showed off a golf-course tan and khaki pants. His smile was confident and relaxed and displayed his perfect teeth.

I studied Brownie's posts again, this time looking at the hashtags she picked. They all said things like #bestlife, #happy, and #luvmylife. The images she displayed to the world were all carefully curated to show that she lived a perfect life with a perfect family. I raised my eyebrows to see a few books included in her posts, along with Brownie rapturously reading. Maybe she just preferred to buy her books instead of finding them in the library. Although I knew I'd seen Brownie at work a handful of times, she definitely wasn't a regular.

My phone rang then, startling me, and I eagerly picked up. It was Grayson and he quickly drove over to pick me up.

"My hero," I said dryly as I climbed into his car.

He grinned at me. "It couldn't have been that bad. You weren't even over there all that long."

"Zelda can be so sour. I was asking her about Greta, and she was espousing that Greta had always been the intended target for the murderer and Esther's death was a mere accident."

Grayson said, "Why would anyone want to kill a retired nurse, except to get rid of a witness?"

"No idea. The police seem pretty positive that Esther's death was no accident. I guess it's just Zelda being Zelda."

Grayson nodded absently and said, "Do you want to drop by my house and grab something to eat? Somehow, I'm starving again."

I accepted his invitation and we settled in the kitchen. Grayson had a quirky style of decorating which was most evident in his kitchen, which showcased his collection of clocks. He had just about every kind of clock there was—cuckoo, pendulum, mantel, and more. We made a couple of grilled cheese sandwiches and canned tomato soup, and I tossed a bag of chips on the table for an instant meal.

Grayson was still mulling over what Zelda had said. "I wonder what Zelda had against Greta."

I snorted inelegantly. "She said Greta was condescending toward her. To me, it speaks more toward Zelda having an unresolved inferiority complex than anything to do with Greta."

"That sounds possible. On a totally different subject, I'm going to try to make it to film club this afternoon. I'm planning on bringing Lars by, too, if I can. He's such a film nut that he needs to come. Plus, he has a real flexible work schedule, like I do."

I raised my eyebrows. "Does Lars *know* he's going?" Lars was about as introverted as I was. He was fine in groups where he knew everyone, but he wasn't as much of a fan of hanging out with a bunch of strangers.

Grayson said, "Oh, he'll be fine. Film club is mostly about the movie anyway. There's not that much time to visit."

I gave him a doubtful look. Film club was definitely more of a community, but I'd let Lars figure that out.

Grayson's doorbell rang and he looked surprised. "I didn't even know anybody knew I was here."

He headed into his living room and opened the door. I frowned. I could see Abby, Grayson's coworker, standing there. Abby always seemed a little too friendly toward Grayson for my comfort level. She'd been dating someone, but I wasn't sure that was still the case. She was a vivacious blonde in her early thirties who enjoyed music and concerts as much as Grayson did. I felt my muscles tense up a little.

"Hi there," chirped Abby. She beamed at me and said, "And hi to you, Ann."

I gave her a smile through my gritted teeth.

"I was just driving by and saw your car here, Grayson. I didn't realize you were coming by the house."

"Ann and I were just grabbing a bite to eat. Her car is on the blink, so I gave her a ride here."

Abby said, "Well, I'm glad I caught up with you. I've been thinking about that concert review you asked me to write."

"That new alternative band? That's tonight, right?"

I had the sudden feeling I knew exactly what was coming.

Sure enough, Abby said, "That's the one. Since it's something totally different from what I usually cover, I was a little worried about the write-up. I want to give the group fair treatment but if I don't really understand what I'm listening to, I might not be the best person to comment on it."

Grayson said, "You want me to handle it?"

"No, I thought you could maybe attend the concert with me? That way I could hear your impressions on the band during the show and what you have to say about it. It might help me out with my perspective the next time I need to tackle a piece on a different music genre."

Grayson nodded. "That sounds like a good idea."

I was clearly the only one who thought it *didn't* sound like a particularly good idea. I wasn't really a jealous sort of person, so I was surprised by my reaction to Abby. Something about her definitely got under my skin. She had that way of showing up at completely unexpected times, which I felt was due a lot more to planning than haphazard meetings. She also only had eyes for Grayson, even if I was the one talking to her. It was very disconcerting.

"Great! That's going to make me feel a lot more confident about writing the story," said Abby brightly. "I'll meet up with you tonight, then. Do you want to go together?"

"No, because I'm not sure what time I'll be able to get away. Let's just meet there."

Abby disappeared as quickly as she'd shown up. I finished eating and said, "I guess I'd better head over to the library."

Grayson said, "Yikes, the time really sneaked up on me. Let me drive you over there." He groaned. "Oh, no. I just told Abby I'd be at that concert tonight, but you need a ride back."

I grinned at him reassuringly because he looked so devastated. "Don't worry—Fitz and I will just have a sleepover at the library."

Grayson snorted. "That actually sounds like something you'd really enjoy. But seriously—how will you get back home?"

"I'll get Luna or Wilson to drive me back. One of them will probably be working late."

"I thought Luna was still riding her bike to work every day," said Grayson.

I shook my head. "She decided she'd rather sleep in the extra few minutes and just drive over. Anyway, I'm sure I can catch a ride with one of them."

We finished up eating and Grayson ran me by my house to pick up Fitz and then head over to the library. It was super-quiet in there, full of people studying and doing research for various projects. There seemed to be a quiet interview taking place at one table. The computer area was full of people using the library's devices. It was busy, but nearly silent, which was unusual.

I took advantage of the lull to finish up the library newsletter, including "Fitz's" advice column. This month, Fitz answered a question about office breakroom etiquette.

The doors to the library opened and an older lady, Cora White, came in. She had snow-white hair clipped securely to the back of her head in an elaborate barrette. I waved to her and she looked around furtively before coming over to see me.

"Is Zelda volunteering here today?" she asked with trepidation.

I shook my head. "She's working today."

I must have looked confused about Cora's concern because Cora quickly said, "Sorry, it's just that I'm trying to avoid Zelda right now. She horned in on my best friend, you know. Totally unacceptable."

"Who is your best friend?"

Cora looked deeply unhappy. "*Was* my best friend. Esther."

Chapter Seven

I blinked at this information. I'd had no idea that Esther and Zelda knew each other, much less that they were friends. It hadn't surprised me that Zelda would steal away someone's best friend, although I was surprised that Zelda had the ability to *make* friends as well as she did. She must be a lot more outgoing with some people than with others.

"Did you know Esther for a long time?" I asked.

Cora nodded. "The two of us had been close since we were teenagers. We'd always listen to records together and go to the high school football games. Small town stuff, you know, but it was fun."

Actually, it sounded quite a bit like my old high school experience in Whitby if you substituted "records" for "music."

I said, "How did Zelda take Esther away from you?"

Cora sighed. "I know complaining about it sounds childish of me, but that's exactly what Zelda did. She horned right in on Esther and was a lot more fun than I was."

I found this very hard to picture, but I nodded sympathetically.

"Zelda likes traveling so they'd go off on day trips together or weekends. I'm the kind of person who likes to sleep in my own bed and doesn't leave Whitby very often," said Cora sadly.

"But getting new friends doesn't mean giving up completely on old friends." Suddenly, an old Girl Scout song on exactly that theme came to mind. My aunt had believed very strongly in the Girl Scouts.

Cora nodded. "The problem was worse than that. I guess I don't respond very well to being pushed away—it makes me become very clingy. So just when Esther was pulling away, I started showing up to see her all the time. Finally Esther got mad and told me I was 'suffocating her.'" Cora looked unhappily down at the library carpet.

I said mildly, "Sometimes friends go through spats like that. I'm sure everything would have ended up being fine if Esther's time hadn't been cut short like it was."

Cora's eyes welled up. "That's the awful thing. Because of our rift, I feel like I can't even mourn Esther like I should. I'm still sort of mad at her for the way she treated me. You see, Esther started saying unpleasant things around town about me and really hurt my feelings."

"What kinds of things?" I frowned.

"Oh, just petty things. Talking about me in a negative way—how I dress, my poor housekeeping habits, my unhealthy diet. Nothing major, but all very hurtful."

I was starting to see why Cora was so upset. It must have felt like a major betrayal. "That must have been awful for you."

Cora nodded, looking miserable. "But then Esther died all of a sudden and I felt terrible about all the mean things I was thinking about her. I couldn't believe she was gone. Every time I'd go by the square, I kept looking for her out of habit. Then things got even *worse*. Well, I guess you know why."

"Because you found out her death wasn't accidental," I said somberly.

"Exactly. And I guess people talked to the police about the falling out between Esther and me because the next thing I knew, Burton was showing up at my door and wanting to talk to me. Can you believe it?" Cora looked very indignant.

"That's just protocol, you know. Burton just has to question everybody to get a more complete picture of what might have happened."

Cora didn't look particularly mollified by my explanation. "I bet I know exactly who told the police that Esther and I were at odds. Zelda. She's really got it in for me."

I didn't reply to this. It did actually sound like something Zelda would do, under the guise of being a good citizen.

"I hope everybody knows that just because Esther and I weren't getting along, I would never have harmed her in any way. We grew up together! I thought of Esther as a sister of mine." A tear slipped down her cheek and she brushed it away. "But I can't help but feel guilty for what happened to Esther, just the same. If I'd just put my foolish pride aside and reconciled with her, maybe she'd still be alive."

I didn't completely follow her line of thought and my confusion must have been evident because Cora continued, "The problem was that Esther knew too many things about people in town. She was outside most of the time because she wasn't crazy about her house or her neighbors. And Esther was *so* observant. She wouldn't just take in everything she saw; she wove it into a story."

I could see Esther doing that—creating a narrative about what she was watching people do. I wondered how accurate her narratives were and if that might have been what got her killed.

Clearly, Cora was thinking along the same terms. She said, "Esther just knew way too many things about people. Things they didn't even realize she knew! If I'd just put my foolish pride aside and reached out to Esther, maybe Esther would have opened up to me and shared whatever she knew."

Cora was tearing up again and I quickly said, "None of this is your fault, Cora. It's just the way things happened. You had no idea Esther was going to be murdered."

"No, you're right. But if Esther *had* talked with me, maybe I could have convinced her to go to the police with whatever she knew. Of course, if she told Zelda about it, then *Zelda* should have told her to call the police."

I had the feeling that Zelda, knowing her, would most certainly have told Esther precisely what to do. Zelda was hardly a shrinking violet and she was very fond of speaking her mind. That made me think that Esther hadn't shared whatever she'd witnessed with Zelda. Was that because Esther hadn't thought it was important? Had she possibly not realized how important whatever she'd witnessed had been?

Cora continued on, "Plus, I feel so terrible about poor Greta. She was a really sweet person. The rumors going around are that the two deaths are connected. Is that what you've heard, too?"

I said carefully, "I'm not really sure. What have you heard?"

"That somebody was trying to hurt Esther earlier and Greta saw it happen. Or maybe that Greta was a witness when Esther was killed. Something like that." Cora shook her head sadly. "I always thought Greta was a lovely person. In fact, I was trying to get to know her better since Esther had fallen out with me. Did you know her at all?"

"She was one of our very capable library volunteers. We did talk with each other, but I wish I'd known her better, too."

Cora said, "Greta used to be a nurse, you know. One of the things that comes with the job is being observant. Esther wasn't the only one—Greta was observant, too. I'm thinking Greta saw something suspicious and then whoever the killer is took her out, too." Cora's face was pink with indignation.

"Do you have any inkling at all as to who might be behind this?"

Cora was solemnly quiet for a few moments, considering the question. "I don't really know anything at all."

Something in her expression, though, made me wonder. It looked to me as if she *did* know something . . . something she'd decided not to share.

I said, "I understand Esther didn't get along too well with her neighbors."

"You can say that again. The problem was all on the neighbors' side, though. The boy has always been rude and loud and his mother is just about as obnoxious. But I can't really see someone murdering a neighbor who complained about noise, can you?"

I shook my head. Then I said, "I was wondering if you knew Esther's motivation in terms of picking up all this information about people. Or *was* there intention and motivation? Was it just information she accidentally learned?"

Cora said, "I think it all started when Esther's husband died. It's been ages ago now. He had a massive aneurism and died right there in her home. They were very close and his death really upset Esther. She couldn't tolerate the house and all the memories she had there of him. So that put her at loose ends. She took to walking at first and would walk all over town most of the day."

"That must have been tiring."

Cora nodded. "It was a little too much. So then she alternated between taking shorter walks and hanging out outdoors at the square. On days with bad weather, she'd sit at the coffee shop until the weather cleared a little and then she'd be back outside. Esther said she enjoyed being outdoors and seeing people. It made her feel part of the community, even if she didn't directly engage with the people she saw. And she sometimes picked up a lot of what was going on around her as a result."

Another patron came in with knitting materials and called out to Cora. She turned and smiled at the woman and said, "I'd better run. See you soon."

As Cora headed away, I saw the library doors swish open again and Mrs. Schubert, the library trustee come in. I could tell she had something on her mind because she seemed to be positively vibrating with indignation.

Sure enough, she came right over to the desk to unload. Some days it felt like I was the equivalent of a bartender or a hairdresser or some other type of professional confidant—and today was definitely one of those days.

"Any tech issues today, Mrs. Schubert?" I asked mildly.

"I only wish my problems were as minor today. I'm absolutely furious with my niece. You won't believe what's happened now."

She seemed to be waiting on me to react, so I gave her an encouraging smile and said, "What's going on with Irene?"

"She got fired from her bank teller job, that's what. Can you believe it? I tell you Ann, I'm at my wit's end. I helped her get that job, you know, because I'm a friend of the bank president. Now I look like a complete idiot for putting my neck out for her."

I said, "I don't think it makes you look like an idiot at all. I think it makes you look like a really devoted aunt who is trying to help your niece find good work."

This mollified Mrs. Schubert a little and she gave me a smile. "I'm trying. I only wish Irene was trying harder on her end. I've been reading that nonfiction book you gave me, by the way. It talks about formulating a plan *before* your dependent asks for handouts. That's what I intend to do. That way I'm not going off pure emotion but follow the policy I've set for myself."

"That sounds like a very smart idea. I'm glad the book has been useful so far. Do you know what happened at the bank? Did Irene just not show up for her shifts?"

Mrs. Schubert's mouth tightened. "She did apparently show up, although punctuality is a recurring problem for her. Apparently, the issue was that her teller window never balanced. The staff would all have to stay after the bank closed to count up her window and see where the discrepancy was. That can only happen a few times before it becomes clear to everyone that it's just not going to work out."

I could imagine that the bank would certainly want to know where its missing money was before everyone could leave for the day. "That must have been scary for Irene, not knowing why her window didn't balance."

Mrs. Schubert waved a dismissive hand. "She said it only happened when the grocery store and the gas station came to her window to make deposits. It got so she avoided the big deposits when she saw them come in—she'd run off for a break. That wasn't good, either." She sighed. "Anyway, I called a friend of mine to do me a favor and get Irene a job at her pet store."

"That was a nice thing to do."

She shrugged. "I still feel a responsibility to my sister, bless her soul, to take care of her daughter. But my patience surely is wearing thin."

She looked over at Wilson's office and saw him put his phone receiver down. "Looks like Wilson is free. I'd better go speak with him about this library board thing."

And with that, she strode off. It was good timing because I needed to get set up for film club. The community room at the library was a great space because it could be converted to anything at the blink of an eye. One minute it could be used for a toddler storytime and the next it was a book club for older adults. For film club, the important tasks were setting up the screen and the popcorn machine. The aroma of popcorn would permeate the entire building, but I thought that made for good advertising for the club.

I was starting to pull out the folding chairs when Grayson came in with his friend Lars. Lars was the quietest of Grayson's friends and I'd felt an immediate connection to him because of his love of books. He didn't usually frequent the libraries, though—he was a second-hand bookshop guy because he was too fond of writing in the margins of his books. That was a practice generally frowned upon in libraries. Lars had a high, academic forehead and a nerdy demeanor.

The guys immediately took over the chair setup. I said, "Lars, I'm glad Grayson was able to persuade you to come."

He smiled at me. "I wanted to see what it was all about. But I'm not sure, just for the record, that I'm ready to commit to watching films as a group activity."

"You like having more input into what you're watching?" I guessed.

Lars considered this. "I think what I said sounds a little snobby in retrospect and I didn't mean for it to be. I'm just not used to consuming my entertainment in group settings."

I chuckled. "So I guess I need to reconsider my invitation to you to join one of our many book clubs at the library."

Grayson's eyes twinkled at me as he continued setting out chairs.

Lars gave me a smile that twisted up one corner of his mouth. "The first thing that came to my mind was a big 'no.' But try and give me a pitch for group consumption of entertainment."

"Okay, I'll give it a go. You know I'm a big reader, like yourself."

Lars nodded.

"What I've noticed, though, in both my reading and my film watching is that I tend to pick specific titles that reflect what I most enjoy or am interested in."

Lars said, "Of course you do. That's only natural—you don't want to waste your time on something you're not going to enjoy."

"That's one facet of it. But when I do that, I find I'm not broadening my perspective in any way. I'm maintaining this sort of echo chamber where I just filter in what I'm interested in. I'm effectively siloed."

Lars was nodding slowly and Grayson had paused with the chairs and was listening, too.

"But when I go to book club, the members suggest novels to read. They often aren't titles I would have chosen but I tend to get a lot out of them." I shrugged. "That's all. Same with film club."

Lars looked thoughtful. "That makes sense. I'll keep that in mind."

I grinned at him. "And while I'm on the topic of different perspectives, if you wanted to come to film club next month, you can propose the movie we watch. We're always looking for something different."

Grayson smiled. "Lars is sure to suggest some sort of obscure art-house film."

I said, "If they're *very* obscure, I might have a tough time getting my hands on them to show them to the group."

Lars said, "There are plenty of great art-house movies that aren't obscure. *Eraserhead* is one. Or maybe *Being John Malkovich*."

I nodded. "That's true. By the way, I'm expecting some more people than usual today. We haven't done a blockbuster for ages and last time someone suggested *E.T.*"

I thought Lars might turn his nose up at the movie, but instead he looked interested. "Wow, I haven't seen that since I was a kid."

I was about to respond to that when most of the film club attendees came in at the same time. Grayson and Lars took a seat while I greeted everyone coming in and made sure folks helped themselves to popcorn.

I noticed there were a lot of new faces there which was exactly what I'd hoped for. I'd done some extra promoting for the club meeting on social media, thinking it might draw in new people. I'd used extra-fetching photos of Fitz with a bag of popcorn and a movie poster of *E.T.* in the background.

The room was charmed when Fitz decided to make an appearance. It was pretty unusual for him to attend because it always occurred during one of his major naptimes when he was zoned out in the breakroom. But this time he seemed alert and happy. Fitz glanced around the room and immediately headed for Grayson and Lars. I assumed he was planning on sitting on Grayson's lap since he knew him so well, but he glided over to Lars instead. Lars looked just as surprised as I felt when Fitz jumped up into his lap and curled up. After a few moments, I saw Lars hesitantly stroke Fitz as Fitz gave him a feline smile.

Timothy, one of my favorite film club members, came into the room. He grinned when he saw me and came over. He was the youngest in our group—a homeschooled teen with a huge love of films.

I said to him, "I was just thinking about you a few minutes ago. I was telling a friend that my goal was always to broaden the scope of what I was reading and writing. It made me think of you. As long as it's a film, you're willing to watch just about anything. Even movies that aren't very good."

He smiled shyly at the implicit compliment. "Thanks. I think I've learned just as much from bad films as I have from good ones."

This, of course, led me to ask what were some of the worst films he'd watched. Timothy didn't even hesitate but started listing them, counting them out on his fingers as he went. "*Howard the Duck*, *Caddyshack II*, *Battlefield Earth*, and *Cats*."

George, a burly film club regular, joined us. "I didn't hear the first part of your conversation, but I sure hope that's a list of the worst films you've ever watched and not what's on the film club calendar."

Timothy and I laughed and Timothy said, "Worst movies ever. Although maybe one day we should have a marathon viewing of bad movies. It might be good for a laugh."

George gave him a wry look. "I don't think I could stomach my popcorn. Your list was good, by the way, but it did have an important omission. *The Room*."

"But that film is so bad, it's good."

That made me laugh again. "I've heard it called the *Citizen Kane* of bad movies."

Timothy said eagerly, "All the better to learn from."

I let George and Timothy argue the point for a few minutes before I said, "Sorry to draw this fascinating debate to a close, but it's time for *E.T.*"

"Now *that's* a good movie," said George with satisfaction.

It was. And it needed little introduction since a show of hands demonstrated everyone in the room had watched it before. Another show of hands, however, indicated that no one had seen it for a long time. I gave a little trivia about the movie, including the fact that the film was mostly shot on a child's eye-level and that *E.T.* had the longest theatrical run, staying in theaters for over a year after its release.

After the movie was over, everyone applauded. Then the discussion started with people listing their favorite parts, talking about the acting, and discussing the suspense in the film. I saw that Lars looked engaged and interested, even if he didn't join in the discussion. I also noticed that Fitz was perfectly content in his lap as Lars absently petted him.

Once the club meeting wrapped up and everyone had taken their conversations out of the room and into the library, I started the cleanup process with Grayson's help. Lars joined in although I said, "Hey, you've done enough. You're a guest, after all."

Lars smiled. "A guest that might very well become a regular. That was actually a lot of fun."

"You didn't mind the group setting?"

Lars considered this. "I think the difference is that I'm comparing it to watching a movie at a movie theater. But the two experiences are completely different. At a movie theater, *anybody* could be there. There are little kids and people who were dragged to the movie who don't even want to be there. But here, everyone is a film enthusiast. They're not talking during the movie or looking at their phone or things like that. The discussion afterwards was pretty interesting, too. So, all-in-all, it added to my enjoyment of the movie."

I smiled at him. "I saw you made a furry friend, too."

"Yeah, he about scared me to death when he suddenly jumped in my lap," said Lars ruefully. "But he's great. He lives here?"

"Well, he spends half his time here and half with me at home. Sort of like me."

Lars nodded. "He's amazing. And I'm not even that much of a cat person." He glanced at his watch. "Okay, I'd better get out of here and get some work done." He nodded at Grayson, who'd given him a wave. "Thanks for the invite."

He walked out and stopped for a second, looking across the library with interest. I moved closer to a window looking out onto the library and saw what he was looking at—Grayson and his mutual friend, Jeremy, talking with great animation to Luna.

Grayson followed my gaze and said, "I see what you were talking about yesterday. They seem to be getting along like a house on fire."

"I know. Part of me is happy for Luna and for Jeremy, too. But I can't help but feel bad for Burton." I paused. "Maybe Luna and Jeremy will just be friends."

But Grayson looked doubtful.

Chapter Eight

After film club, Grayson left for work again and I settled back at the reference desk. Jeremy came over with a book to check out.

He grinned happily at me. "Recommended by Luna. She thought I might like it."

I checked out *Zen and the Art of Motorcycle Maintenance* for him. "It's a great book. Kind of quirky."

"Like Luna," he said approvingly. "She has another one for me after this. *House of Leaves.*"

"Another very unconventional read." You could really learn a lot about a person from the books they read. Jeremy didn't seem nearly as quirky as Luna was, but opposites definitely attracted sometimes.

"I saw I just missed Lars," Jeremy said. "Was that the film club I've been hearing about from Grayson?"

I nodded. "You should give it a go if you enjoy movies. We've got a great group."

He looked thoughtful. "I may have to try it out. It would give me the chance to catch up with Grayson and Lars, too." But he was looking toward the children's section and Luna as he said it. "Actually," he added, "is there a list of library events that I could take home with me? It looks like I've been missing out on a lot over here."

I handed him a printed copy of the library newsletter. "More events are added all the time, so be sure to check online for updates."

After Jeremy left, I was busy for a while. Students had headed over to the library after class let out to work on research and group projects and they kept me hopping asking me questions and looking for resources.

Burton came in shortly after things started settling down. I smiled at him and he came over to the desk.

"How is everything going with the case?" I asked.

He sighed. "I guess it's all right, but nothing is as straightforward as it looks. We basically have two unexplained deaths that are somehow connected, one of which was considered an accident for a while. With Esther's death, it's tough to pinpoint exactly when it occurred on the day in question. Anyway, I was wondering if you had any information to share. I know folks in the community come in here and share things with you—have you heard any local gossip?"

I said, "Actually, I had the chance to speak with Freddie Jenkins directly because Grayson is doing a piece on Esther. Then, on the way out, we spoke with Esther's neighbors."

Burton raised his eyebrows. "You've made quite a bit of headway, then. What were your impressions?"

"Freddie didn't seem all that shaken up by his mother's death although I know everyone reacts to grief differently."

Burton nodded. "He did seem very focused on clearing out his mom's house so he could move in."

"Exactly. He seemed like the kind of person who likes to live big and maybe beyond his means. He was very proud of his new car. I wondered if he had a lot of debt and was looking forward to paying it off with his mom's money. I was also surprised to hear that Esther had a good deal of money. She definitely wasn't the kind of person to be flashy with it. Esther seemed to live very simply and not spend very much."

Fitz came over to say hi to Burton and the policeman rubbed him absently as the cat purred in delight. "So you got the impression money might have been a motive."

I shrugged. "Freddie denied any responsibility and made sure Grayson took notes to that effect. He seemed to realize people might be talking about him."

Burton grunted. "Right. And you said you spoke to the neighbors, too? I'm guessing you spoke with Brownie."

"And her son, Lyle."

Burton chuckled. "That must have been a treat. Was Lyle in his usual, surly mood?"

"Well, I'm not really sure what constitutes as normal for Lyle. I have the feeling it was probably his usual mood, though. He didn't seem to like Esther very much."

"I'm sure he didn't," said Burton. "I have a bunch of complaints about Lyle on file—all from Esther."

"I got the impression it was just normal teenager stuff, though? Being loud?"

Burton nodded. "That's really what it was. His music, his band . . . that kind of stuff. How was Brownie?"

"Protective over Lyle, which I totally understand. But she was also at odds with Lyle because she wanted to take a selfie with him and he wanted nothing to do with it."

Burton said, "It's got to be tough living with Brownie. Lyle has my sympathy. He can't just slouch in the picture and look hostile. I've looked at her social media and she's trying to present a picture to the world of a perfect family."

"I think the family is probably pretty far from perfect, like most families are. I did want to tell you that Brownie did mention they'd tried to buy Esther's property from her to expand their house."

Burton raised an eyebrow. "Expand *that* house?"

"I guess it feels small to them."

Burton sighed. "Well, that's yet another statement on how the family gets along—they need even more room to escape each other." He paused. "Of course, Esther turned them down. She didn't need the money and the house meant something to her, even if she didn't spend much time there."

"Brownie didn't seem to realize she was listing another reason she might want Esther dead. After all, if she tries to negotiate a sale with Freddie, he might be happy to take the money and run."

Burton grunted. "Yeah. Money talks to that guy. He's happy to take his mom's house for free, but he'd be just as happy to get paid off and buy something much bigger and better." He glanced over to the children's section. "Do you think Luna is busy right now? Any storytimes or anything like that, or can I run over and say hi?"

"She doesn't have anything going on right now." I watched a little sadly as Burton eagerly walked over to spend some time with Luna.

When my shift was over, I found Luna, who was also getting ready to leave. "Can you give me a ride over to the garage? My car was acting up but it should be fixed now. Plus, they're about to close for the day."

"Sure thing," said Luna, looking a little preoccupied and quieter than usual.

I knew something was wrong when I realized I was making small talk during the ride to the garage. There was never any small talk around Luna. She was either giving an enthusiastic monologue about whatever she was thinking about, or speaking her mind about a big issue of the day.

"Is everything okay?" I asked.

Luna nodded and then stopped. She shook her head. "Not really, Ann." She looked uncomfortable. "I feel kind of weird talking about it with you, though. You're friends with Burton, after all."

"But I'm also friends with *you*."

Luna nodded again. "You're right." She took a deep breath. "Okay, here we go. I think I want to date someone else."

She pulled into a parking space at the garage and turned to look at me. "But I don't want to hurt Burton at all. He's such a great guy, like I was saying earlier. He deserves more than this lopsided relationship we're in."

I said slowly, "I don't have a lot of experience with relationships, but I know you don't have a commitment to Burton. The two of you aren't married, Luna. Breaking up with someone when the relationship isn't working out is what it's all about, isn't it? It's a lot fairer to Burton to let him know and give him the opportunity to find someone who's better suited for him."

"You're right. Of course you're right. I just hate to do it, that's all." Luna groaned. "Why does everything have to be so hard?" She stared out the windshield of her car blankly. Then she turned to look at me again. "I guess you know who I'm interested in going out with."

I nodded. "I could see that you and Jeremy were really hitting it off. Do the two of you have a lot in common?"

Luna looked wryly at me. "It doesn't seem likely, does it? I'm a children's librarian and he does something . . . well, I really don't even know what he does. Some kind of corporate sales or something?"

I shook my head. "No idea. All I know is that he has a tough time focusing at home sometimes and that's the whole reason he was in the library to begin with."

Luna continued, "And then there's a really big age difference between us. Ugh."

"You wouldn't think it was a big difference if *he* were the one who was older."

Luna considered this and then smiled. "You're right. It's just weird because I'm the older one."

I was quiet for a moment and then said, "You've been listing all the things you *don't* have in common. But I could see there was a real spark between the two of you."

A smile tugged at the corners of her mouth again. "He seems like a great guy. I know you don't know anything about his job, but do you know anything about *him*?"

"Only that he seems like a really nice guy. He's laid-back and friendly and gets along great with Grayson." I frowned, trying to come up with some more details. "Sadly, that's about all I know. I only met him myself not very long ago."

Luna said, "What do you think I should do? I mean, I know you said I should level with Burton and I totally agree. But besides that?" She hesitated. "Do you think you could find out from Grayson if Jeremy is interested in me at all? I don't want to make a fool of myself by breaking up with Burton to go out with a guy who has no plans on asking me out."

I winced. "I don't know, Luna. Isn't that a little . . . ."

"Third grade?" asked Luna wryly.

"I'm happy to help you out but I think it would be better if you see how things evolve with Jeremy first. Unless you want to break up with Burton on other grounds."

Luna tilted her head to one side, her purple hair dangling. "That might be better. If I break up with Burton because I want to see someone else, it seems like that would be more hurtful than telling him that I want to be just friends." She scowled. "Although that's such a hackneyed phrase. Maybe I should just say that he deserves someone better than me?"

I gave her a doubtful look.

"Yeah, that's not good either."

I said, "I'm sure you'll end up saying just the right thing. After all, you care about Burton."

Luna nodded glumly. "Exactly. That's what makes this so hard."

She drove away with a thoughtful expression on her face as I walked into the garage to pick up my car.

The next morning, I woke up with Fitz standing on my chest and looking meaningfully into my eyes. When he saw my eyes open, he started purring.

"Gosh, what time is it, Fitz?" I asked in a husky, just-woken-up voice. I squinted at the clock. No wonder he'd been ready to wake me up. It was eight o'clock. I guess I'd needed to catch up on my sleep. It was a good thing I was off for the day.

The phone rang and I nearly dropped it in my hurry to answer before it went to voicemail. "Grayson?" I asked in that same early-morning croak.

"Hey there. Is everything okay?"

I cleared my throat and gave a dry laugh. "It's all fine. I just woke up."

"Really?"

Grayson sounded stunned and I laughed again.

"Really. I'm just as surprised as you are. Fitz had to resuscitate me this morning. I woke up only because he was pawing at me. I think he might have been concerned and was checking to make sure I was still breathing."

Grayson said, "I was going to suggest we go out for a run in the park, but I have the feeling that's going to be a little too active right now for you."

"Yeah, I think so. If I'd been up for longer than just a few minutes I think I could have risen to the occasion."

"No problem," said Grayson. "What are your plans for today?"

I considered this for a moment, trying to focus even though the fog of sleep was still hanging around me. Fitz looked at me with interest and I said, "I might head over to the pet store to pick up some cat food. I'm running pretty low. Plus, I found out yesterday that Irene Bell works there. Her aunt is a patron of mine and she's been pretty worried about Irene lately."

"You know her?" asked Grayson.

I said dryly, "Remember, I know practically everyone in town on some level. It comes from living in a small town most of your life. I do know Irene and thought I might check in on her."

"What's made her aunt so worried?"

"Maybe *worried* is the wrong word. Mrs. Schubert is more irritated or annoyed. But I think the underlying feeling is worry. Her sister died when Irene was a young teen and she took over Irene's care. Irene seems like she has a hard time sticking with anything—she dropped out of her expensive college and then has had a tough time holding down a job."

"Got it. Sounds like she isn't really sure what she wants . . . she's more sure of what she *doesn't* want."

I said, "Exactly. Anyway, that's what I've got on tap for today. How about you?"

Grayson said rather darkly, "Well, I've already had to deal with emailing my photographer a counter-offer."

"Oh no. Brownie already tried to steal him away? That was fast."

"That's right. She was offering pretty good money for part time work."

I said, "But he probably knew it was better to work for a newspaper than a social media influencer. Folks like Brownie could be here today and gone tomorrow."

Grayson sighed. "Some people think newspapers are the same way."

"But newspapers aren't reliant on a single person, either. Brownie could really mess up and say or do the wrong thing and her whole social media profile could fall like a house of cards. Were you able to convince your photographer to stay on?"

"I was, thank goodness. But it was touch and go for a while. Anyway, I should get on with it—hope you have a good morning, Ann."

I had breakfast and then, feeling a little guilty that I hadn't gone for a run with Grayson, took out some hand weights and did some stretches with them. After that I got ready and headed out of the house.

The pet store used to be a private home that was built in the 1930s. It had tons of character and was a fun place to shop. The wooden floors were warped enough that you had to watch your step walking up the mini hills and valleys. The walls were covered with jaunty paintings of dogs and cats—sometimes dressed up in human clothing and in unlikely settings. There were also photos of the shop's customers scattered around the store. The different rooms had toys, food, beds, and more. The owner lived above the store. I kept thinking that I'd have to bring Fitz in one day, but I hadn't yet. Although he was very much at ease at both my house and the library, I wondered if introducing a new place to him (one that usually had several dogs in it) might be a little stressful for him.

Irene was sitting at a desk behind the cash register, looking a little bored and maybe a bit discontented. She had a weak mouth and mousy brown hair and she slumped as she sat. I noticed she had earbuds in her ears and was probably listening to music because she was swaying as she sat. She didn't notice I'd come in and I didn't want to startle her, so I moved carefully into her line of vision. Irene looked surprised and took out one of her earbuds.

Chapter Nine

"Hey Ann, how's everything going?" she asked.

"Just fine. I thought I'd pick up some food for Fitz."

Irene sometimes came into the library, so she knew who Fitz was. She said, "Aw, you didn't bring him?"

I shook my head. "I'm never sure how he'd handle it, so I just leave him."

"That's too bad. Visiting with people's pets is the only part of this job that's any fun at all. I was about to die of boredom by myself before you came in."

She put her earbud back in and I found Fitz's cat food. I also wandered through the cat toy section. Since I'm permanently on a budget, I usually make homemade toys for Fitz. This time, though, I was tempted by the ones on display. I winced as I saw the prices, but figured I could buy one of them, anyway, since I'd saved so much in the past by making toys.

I walked up to the checkout counter and smiled at Irene. She pulled out both earbuds this time and said in a rote voice, "Find what you're looking for?"

I nodded. "Are you new here? I don't think I've seen you here before."

"Yeah. I was working over at the bank but that didn't really work out." Irene said this completely casually as if jobs not working out was a common occurrence. Which it sounded like it was, according to her aunt. She sighed. "I really would like to get out of Whitby altogether. Wouldn't you? We've both been here since we were little kids."

"I actually really like it here," I said slowly. "But I know a lot of people I went to school with have moved away."

Irene said, "Exactly. I want to see the world, you know? There's so much out there besides Whitby and I feel like the clock is ticking. I don't just want to go to the major tourist areas, either. I mean, of *course* I want to see London, Paris, and Rome, but I'd also really like to go to some offbeat areas like Iceland or Costa Rica. Places like that. I'd like to go to some *real* restaurants, not just Quittin' Time." She gave me a curious look. "How are you so happy here? You spend a lot of time just at the library, don't you? Plenty of people do, of course. My aunt is there *all* the time."

I shrugged. "Maybe I just find adventure in the everyday. Plus, with all the books I read, I'm an experienced armchair traveler."

Irene said wryly, "Different strokes for different folks. Anyway, I can talk about leaving Whitby, but here I am stuck at a pet shop. This is better for me than the bank, though. I really couldn't stand being a teller—it seemed like a ton of pressure for a job that didn't pay great. I like hanging out with the animals here. And the shop is pretty cheerful."

It was. Besides all the happy pet décor, there was sunlight streaming through every window.

I said, "I know that most of the folks who come into the library feel the same way. They seem to enjoy petting Fitz while they're studying or checking out books. He helps people to de-stress."

"I really need to get back into reading books. I used to like reading when I was little but then I guess I just fell out of the habit. What are you reading now?"

I smiled at her. "A great book by Daphne du Maurier—*Rebecca*. Have you read it? Or maybe watched the movie?"

Irene shook her head and I continued, "It's got this great gothic feel to it. A young woman from meager means met a rich man. They marry and he moves her to his family home which is very isolated, dark, and gloomy. His housekeeper only wants to talk about the previous wife, Rebecca, and how amazing she was. Things get very creepy from there."

"You make it sound really good," said Irene thoughtfully.

I shrugged. "It's no-risk entertainment because you can check it out from the library for free."

"I'll have to run by there." Irene glanced idly out of the shop window and suddenly froze. I followed her gaze and saw Burton passing by. He continued walking and Irene relaxed again.

She gave me a rueful look. "Isn't that crazy? I keep acting like I'm being hunted down or something."

"Why do you feel that way?" It was a strong reaction, even though I knew Irene had, from all reports, engaged in a bit of shoplifting. Had that made her leery of the police all the time though? Even when she wasn't doing anything wrong?

Irene said, "I don't know. The way Burton was talking, he's acting like I have something to do with the deaths of those two older women."

I must have looked confused because Irene continued, "He talked to me to find out where I was when they died. I blame my aunt for that. I bet she said something to Burton about me. She's just sick and tired of having to help me out all the time. She'd probably rather have me locked up and out of the way in jail."

I said slowly, "I see your aunt in the library pretty regularly and I haven't gotten that impression at all from her. She always seems genuinely concerned about how you're doing." Frustrated, too. Definitely annoyed. But I hadn't gotten the feeling that she wished any harm on Irene whatsoever. If anything, all her actions pointed to her desire to help Irene for her dead sister's sake.

Irene looked a little abashed. "You're right. I'm just saying that because we're both kind of irritated with each other right now. My aunt wants to help me but she doesn't care at all about what *I* want. She just wants me in a safe, boring job and here in Whitby for the rest of my life. She's not interested in the fact that I want something more exciting. If I lived in New York, there'd be a lot more kinds of jobs that I could pick and choose from."

And a much higher cost of living. I managed to keep that opinion to myself, though.

"And if I lived in New York, maybe I could actually meet somebody and be in some kind of relationship. You know there aren't a lot of guys here to choose from."

I nodded wryly. I had the feeling I'd dated twenty percent of the available population of Whitby before Grayson moved into town. I said, "You and your aunt sound like you've just got two totally different perspectives of your future."

"Exactly. I'm not saying I'm not grateful to her for helping me out. My mom was a single mom and after she died, I don't know what would have happened to me if my aunt hadn't taken me in and raised me. I guess I would have gone into foster care or something. Anyway, she did a good job bringing me up—I'm a good citizen. Most of the time."

"When the police were talking to you about the deaths of the two women, did you have an alibi at all?"

Irene shrugged. "Not really. They didn't really know when one of them died and I was working at the bank then which is on the square. For the other lady, I was off that day and didn't spend the day with anybody. Apparently, there are only mysterious deaths when I'm not on full public display somewhere." She paused. "I didn't even know who these women were that they were talking about."

"You'd never met Esther or Greta?" I asked.

"Why would I? I mean, maybe I met them while I was working at the bank or something, but it's not like I would even have had a conversation with them or anything. It's not like they were friends of mine. I don't know what the cops are thinking."

A big, rather dopey looking dog came lolling over and Irene crooned, "Bobo! Hey there, sweetie. Did you wake up from your nap?"

Bobo looked as if he'd barely woken up enough to really even walk closer to Irene. Instead, he threw himself on his back in the hopes of getting a tummy rub. Irene quickly acquiesced and so did I. Although Bobo didn't seem to be the brightest animal in the world, he certainly seemed like a sweetheart.

"Is Bobo yours?" I asked as I rubbed the dog's belly.

She shook her head. "He belongs to the owner who lives over the shop. He's the shop dog, like Fitz is the library cat. He's a sweet guy but doesn't help me out with my boredom much because he sleeps all day." She frowned. "What were we talking about?"

"About Greta and Esther."

Irene threw her hands up in the air. "Yeah, that's another reason why I'm ready to leave town. It's so small here that everybody falls under suspicion when there's a mysterious death."

"Do you have any concrete plans for moving away from Whitby?" I asked.

"Not yet. I read blog posts and stuff, though to find out more information. I read a lot about New York, for instance. I've figured out how you can connect with potential roommates online. I just have to keep putting money in my piggybank to make it happen."

Although I believed Irene did truly want to leave Whitby and head off for a more exciting life, she sounded like the kind of person who talked a big game but never actually ended up following through. Plus, it looked like she'd picked up quite an expensive coffee at Keep Grounded, if the whipped cream and the sweet smell coming from the cup were anything to go by.

Irene stood up again and Bobo promptly fell asleep where he lay on the floor.

"I wonder if Burton would even let me leave town right now. Do they let suspects go?"

I shook my head. "I don't really know. Did he warn you not to?"

"No. Anyway, I could always leave him with a forwarding address, couldn't I? That's something I've seen them do on those police dramas. It's a waste of his time to be thinking about me as a suspect since I had nothing to do with it. He could be spending time actually tracking down the real killer."

"And you don't have any idea who that might be?" I asked.

A flicker of annoyance crossed Irene's features. "Why would I? I didn't know them, remember?" She glanced at the toy and the food I was holding in my hands. "Are you ready to check out?"

After walking out with my purchases, I was just getting into my car when a woman called out to me. I looked up and recognized the older lady as one of my patrons from the library.

"Hi, Mrs. Tilton," I said. "How are you doing?"

"Oh, fine, fine," she said in a breathless voice. "I'm glad I caught up with you. I've been meaning to run by the library, but just haven't had the chance."

She reached into her voluminous purse and pulled out a paperback book—one of ours from the library. I blinked at her.

"Could you return this for me?" asked the older lady sweetly. "I know for sure you'll be there at some point and likely before I'll be able to make it over."

I slowly took the book from her.

"You're a doll!" she said and scampered away.

Back home again, I played with Fitz for a while, to his excitement. It was one of those fishing line type of toys—a stick attached to a string and a dangling furry-looking doll that was meant to resemble prey of some kind. The fake prey also made chittering sounds that made Fitz positively wild. He kept pouncing on the creature until he wore himself out and trotted over to a sunbeam.

I picked up *Rebecca* and curled up on the sofa. I read happily for the next couple of hours, then decided I probably needed to get some stuff done around the house. Housework was never my favorite thing to do, but I could make myself more enthusiastic about it if I created a list of things I needed to accomplish. That way, I could tick off the items as I completed them. It was silly, but it gave me a sort of rush. Much more of a rush than cleaning for cleaning's sake did.

I played music while I worked. To prove to myself that I could enjoy new music as much as Grayson and Abby, I streamed a band that he'd recently recommended to me. I didn't think it was the kind of music I could sit still and listen to for very long, but it worked very well as clean-up music.

Afterwards, I decided to jump into another chore that I never looked forward to—meal prep. Since my schedule at the library meant that I could be working until nine p.m. some nights, it made sense to have meals ready for me to eat when I came home. There was also the matter of preparing healthy lunches for the breakroom at the library. Eating out was all well and good, but I didn't have the money to do it regularly.

Before I knew it, it was dinnertime. I called up Grayson to see if he wanted to come by and partake in some of the stir-fry I'd just put together.

"Hey there," he said warmly when he picked up the phone. "I was just thinking about you."

"Same," I said with a smile. "I was just wondering if you wanted to walk over and eat supper with me."

"Ordinarily I'd love to, but for some reason, I'm totally wiped out tonight. Maybe I need to catch up on my sleep or something. Can I take a rain check?"

I said, "Of course you can. Hope you can get some good sleep tonight."

He chuckled. "We'll see. I've been yawning so much that I'm not sure I can stay up until eight. Then I'll probably be up around two and won't be able to fall back asleep."

"Early to bed and early to rise."

He said wryly, "We'll see. I'm not sure if it's automatically going to follow that I'll be healthy, wealthy, and wise, no matter what Ben Franklin said."

I ended up turning in pretty early, myself, which meant I started the day early. I was able to do some floor exercises and light weights before eating breakfast and getting ready. Fitz and I got to the library about forty-five minutes before it opened. Mornings were always my favorite time of day there. Light poured in through the windows, illuminating the houseplants we'd set out. It was quiet and the day always seemed to hold such promise. Fitz curled up on the reference desk with his fluffy tail covering his eyes and nose and fell right asleep.

Wilson was always looking for ways to engage the community so I spent a little time on the computer looking to see what other libraries were doing in that regard. My favorite was a book bingo game one library had come up with. The idea was that patrons would try to complete their bingo cards that were filled out with challenges like "a short book (*Tuesdays with Morrie, Driving Miss Daisy, Candide*)", "an international book (*The Little Prince, The Shadow of the Wind, Like Water for Chocolate*)", and "a book with non-human characters (*Watership Down*, *Charlotte's Web*, *The Art of Racing in the Rain*)". I wondered if I should adapt it to have a library version of it: patrons would take an online computer class with us or download a magazine or book online. Or maybe I could create both a book bingo and a library one.

I was still stewing over the details when Wilson came in. I could always tell Wilson's mood by the way he was dressed. If he was feeling more relaxed, he'd come in without a jacket—just his button-down and tie. If he was feeling jaunty, he'd have the jacket slung over his shoulder by his finger. If he was in a somber mood, the jacket would be on and he'd look as if he'd put on armor for the day.

Today, he was relaxed. That made *me* relaxed.

"Hi, Ann. How are things going this morning?" He peeped over the reference desk and Fitz lifted his head lazily and gave a trill. Wilson reached over to rub him.

"Everything is good. Fitz and I got the computers running and everything set for the day. I've found something we might want to try for community engagement."

Wilson now looked even perkier. "Have you? I thought our program calendar was too full."

"That's what is so nice about this particular bit of outreach—it's not a program. It's book bingo. I thought I might also create a library bingo to help patrons become more comfortable with our services."

Wilson said slowly, "I see. And you could share it on social media, I suppose. Patrons would want to complete their bingo card and get . . .?"

I shrugged. "Recognition online? A picture with Fitz? Candy? All of the above?"

Wilson was liking this plan even more since the prizes didn't involve travel mugs, gift cards, or tote bags. "That sounds like a great idea, Ann."

"I'll design the bingo cards today and let you take a look before I share them on our social."

"Sounds good. I'm going out to lunch with Mona today, but that's all that I have on my calendar."

"Quittin' Time?" I asked with a grin. Whitby didn't have many different options.

Wilson's nose wrinkled a little at the mention of the decades-old Whitby establishment. "I believe we're going to try that new restaurant and see how it is."

"Let me know. They just opened, didn't they?"

Wilson nodded. "I spotted white tablecloths through the front window, so it might be a slightly higher-end experience."

That was a low bar to reach since Quittin' Time was hardly fancy.

Wilson headed off to his office and I worked on the draft for the bingo cards. Shortly before the library opened, I gave Grayson a quick call just to check in. His phone went right to voicemail, which was surprising. I looked at the time again and figured maybe he was in an early work meeting. Then I got up to unlock the library doors and welcome the patrons who were already standing there.

The morning was something of a blur of activity and, before I knew it, Wilson and Mona were heading out for lunch.

Wilson frowned and looked at the clock over the desk. "Isn't it time for you to be going to lunch, Ann?"

Mona gave me a wry smile. Wilson was very much the manager, even when it came to taking our breaks. This was ironic since he was also the one who provided the heavy workload for me. He was always coming up with new ways to keep me busy.

"She may not be hungry quite yet," said Mona.

Wilson's brows knit. "Nonsense. She was here when I arrived this morning and, from all appearances, had been at the library for a long while. Ann *must* be hungry."

"I just lost track of time, that's all," I said. "Don't worry—I'll go ahead and take my break now."

I headed into the breakroom and pulled my lunch out of the fridge. Suddenly, thinking about Wilson's and Mona's lunch outing, I wished I'd been more creative with my own lunch offering. It was a salad and I liked all the veggies I'd included but somehow, having a cold lunch just didn't seem very appealing.

I remembered I hadn't heard back from Grayson and rang him again. I was startled to hear a feminine voice pick up his phone on the fourth ring. "Grayson's phone," said the brisk voice on the other end.

Chapter Ten

I paused, then said, "Uh . . . this is Ann. Who am I speaking with?"

"Oh, hi Ann. It's Abby."

"Hi there." I was very confused about why Grayson wasn't answering his phone and why Abby had suddenly stepped into that role. "Could I speak with Grayson?"

"He can't talk right now. He called in sick to the office this morning and so I decided to run by and check on him. He's sleeping now, which is probably the best thing for him."

There was just the slightest bit of censure in her voice, as if I should have thought to do that.

"I didn't realize he was sick," I said slowly. "What's wrong? Do I need to arrange to take him to the doctor?"

Abby quickly answered, "No, there's no need to take off work. I know you run on a tight schedule over at the library."

I pressed my lips together. Was Abby rubbing her job's flexibility in my face? I decided I was reading too much into all this. "So it's nothing he needs to get an antibiotic for?"

Abby said, "It's just a bad migraine. He'll probably feel a lot better once he wakes up."

"Can you get him to call me when he does?"

"Of course," said Abby coolly.

Of course. But somehow I wasn't altogether convinced Abby had my best interests at heart or would even pass along a simple phone message. I ate my cold salad with even less enthusiasm than I'd mustered when I'd first pulled it out of the breakroom fridge. I ate quickly, not feeling like lingering over lunch.

I took only a fraction of my lunch break and installed myself behind the reference desk when someone called my name and I saw Jeremy standing there.

"How's it going?" I asked. "Did your project go okay?"

He looked momentarily confused.

"You know—the project you came to the library to work on," I said.

Jeremy chuckled. "Oh, *that* project. Yes, it went fine, thanks. Working here was a good idea. I guess I have other things on my mind today and that's why I didn't follow you."

"Everything okay?" I asked.

Jeremy suddenly looked a little shy. "Yeah. Things seem to be going really well. That's what I wanted to ask you about."

He glanced over toward the children's section and I said, "Luna's actually off today. If you were looking for her, I mean."

He flushed a bit. "I figured. I just thought I'd ask you about Luna, if you don't mind." He rubbed his face. "Geez, this is awkward."

That made me laugh. "I know what you mean. Between you and Luna, I feel as if I've suddenly been transported back to school and I'm passing notes in class."

"So she's been asking about me, too?" Jeremy's face lit up.

I nodded. "She said something about feeling a real connection with you."

A warm glow settled over Jeremy's features. "So she's not dating anyone?"

I held up my hands. "I didn't say that. She's actually been seeing someone for a while now. You'll have to speak with her about that."

It almost made me smile to see how comically Jeremy's face fell to the totally crestfallen point. "It's a serious relationship?"

"Well, they're not married or anything, no. And Luna might have plans to end their relationship, but again, that's something you'll need to speak with her about."

"End the relationship because of me?" Jeremy seemed pleased by this idea.

"And probably some other reasons. But most pressingly, you."

Jeremy paused for a few minutes. "Who is she dating, if you don't mind me asking?"

"Burton Edison."

Jeremy rubbed his face again, looking so woebegone he made me smile. "The police chief. Fantastic."

"Burton is a great guy, you know." I liked Jeremy . . . actually, I liked all of Grayson's friends, which definitely made life a lot easier. But I'd known Burton longer and felt a strange loyalty to him.

"Oh, I know, I know. He's super-nice. But getting on the wrong side of the police chief in a small town isn't exactly my idea of a good time."

I said briskly, "Just remember that's not your problem. It's ultimately up to Luna to decide what she wants to do and if she's looking to end that relationship."

Jeremy's mouth twisted into a wry smile. "Good point, Ann. You're a very sensible person."

I said, "Don't be too impressed. I can definitely get off-track, too."

Jeremy quirked a brow. "Everything okay with Grayson?"

"I'm sure it is."

I must have sounded less-than-convincing because Jeremy quirked both brows now. "What's going on?"

I took a deep breath and was able to say in a very low-key manner, "Probably nothing. I found out a little while ago that Grayson had called in sick for work this morning."

"Sorry to hear that. That's kind of surprising—I don't think I ever remember Grayson being sick. The rest of us will have colds and Grayson stays infuriatingly above the fray. Is he okay?"

"Well, Abby answered his phone and said he had a migraine."

Jeremy's very animated eyebrows shot up again. "Wait—Abby from work?"

I nodded and he gave a low whistle. "Abby from work was at his house?"

"She said she went over there after he called in sick at work. To check on him." I shrugged.

Jeremy quickly said, "Yeah, I'm sure that says more about Abby than it does about Grayson. I know from the couple of times I've had migraines that all I wanted to do was sleep. He might not even be aware she's over there. Maybe she let herself in."

"Maybe." Although the thought that Abby had a key to Grayson's place, coworker or no coworker, was even more disturbing.

Jeremy said, "Just don't worry about it. You know how crazy Grayson is about you. You're all he talks about. He clearly has no interest in Abby at all." He glanced at his watch and grimaced. "Okay, I'd better be cracking or I'm going to find myself out of a job. Good talking to you, Ann."

I tried jumping back into work, but I found myself not only totally distracted but also dragging. That was the problem with waking up early—sometimes it was tough to sustain the momentum. Then I'd end up turning in early tonight, waking up early tomorrow, and the cycle would continue. I considered my options. One option was to retreat again to the breakroom, taking a nap in there for the rest of the lunch break I hadn't taken. The only problem with that is naps could make me very groggy. The last thing I wanted was to wake up feeling even sleepier than I did now.

The other option was to run out and get some high-octane coffee from Keep Grounded. I knew the coffee in the breakroom wasn't strong (Wilson was a fan of weak coffee) so heading over there was the best way to get a caffeine infusion. I glanced at the clock.

I stuck my head into Wilson's office since he'd recently returned from his lunch break. "I'm going to pop out really quick to Keep Grounded and pick up a coffee to go."

Wilson, who'd been peering closely at what looked like a tremendous pile of spreadsheets, gave me a vague look. "Coffee? Don't we have a pot in the breakroom?"

"I think I probably need something a little stronger to do the trick today. I'm practically nodding off at the reference desk.

Can I pick you up something over there? A latte? Mocha? I'm going to have an espresso."

Wilson shook his head. "I'd be climbing the walls if I had something with a lot of caffeine in it. Thanks, though." He pushed his glasses further up his nose and was absorbed by the spreadsheets again.

I quickly headed out to the coffeehouse. It was a quick walk, just past the square. Because it was after the lunch rush, the street outside was very quiet and no one was sitting in the square. I thought again about Esther and how everyone was used to seeing her and perhaps didn't think much about it because she was a fixture there. I wondered if she would have appreciated being spoken to by people and wished again that I'd taken the time to be more outgoing.

A bell rang as I walked in through the coffeehouse's door but I didn't immediately see anyone at the counter. I knew sometimes it was just Rufus working there, covering everything himself. I waited at the counter for a minute, thinking he might be out back with an incoming delivery or even putting the trash out in the alley's dumpster.

When no one came after a minute, though, I started getting a little antsy. I was going to have to walk back to the library with no coffee at all if no one showed up soon. I called out, "Hello? Rufus? Tara? Anybody here?"

I didn't hear anything, so I walked back out the door and headed around the back of the shop to the alleyway.

That's when I spotted a figure slumped in front of the dumpster.

Chapter Eleven

I realized I was holding my breath, standing frozen, which wasn't helpful for anyone. I hurried over to the figure, who I now realized was Rufus Mitchell. I put my hand on the side of his neck, feeling for a pulse. There was a very weak one so I called 911. The dispatcher walked me through doing chest compressions while I had my phone on speaker. I was grateful for the help because, although I was certified as all of us in the library were, I wanted to make sure I was doing everything right.

It looked like Rufus had a massive head injury, which I also mentioned to dispatch after I saw it in the dim light of the alley. They advised me not to move him so I left him where he was. After a few minutes, I heard an ambulance siren, which made waves of relief pour over me.

Then I heard a bloodcurdling scream from behind me. I turned to see Brownie standing there, looking absolutely appalled at the scene in front of her.

"What did you do to him?" asked Brownie, gaping at me as I crouched over Rufus.

"Do you know CPR?" I gritted through my teeth. Because doing CPR is completely exhausting.

She nodded wordlessly. "I'm certified."

I gestured to Rufus and she immediately took over as the siren grew closer and the emergency workers finally reached us.

I gave the EMTs what little information I had, and they quickly took Rufus away in the ambulance, its siren continuing to blare on the way to the hospital.

Then I took out my phone with a shaking hand.

"Who are you calling?" demanded Brownie, still acting as if she was suspicious of my motives.

"The police," I muttered before the call connected to Burton.

I filled him in quickly and then, suddenly exhausted, headed for the coffeehouse.

"Wait! Aren't you going to tell me what's going on?"

I said, "If you follow me inside. I want to sit down."

And sit down I did—plopped down was more like it since it felt as if my legs weren't enthusiastic about supporting me anymore. Then, making Brownie wait again, I quickly called Wilson, told him what happened, and explained that I'd be speaking with Burton.

Brownie was giving me an impatient look. "Well?"

Suddenly, she seemed very annoying to me. "What were *you* doing in the alley, Brownie?" I asked.

She flushed, pushing her hair back off her shoulders. "I came in here looking for a cup of coffee. Since nobody was here, I went around back to see what the holdup was."

"Same," I offered coolly.

"So you *found* Rufus like that?" she asked.

I nodded.

I was relieved to see Burton come in just a few moments later. Quick police response was one of the nice things about living in a small town.

He gave me a sympathetic look. "How are you holding up, Ann?"

I said ruefully, "Well, I'm awake now. The whole reason I came over here was because I was practically falling asleep at work. That's not going to be a problem anymore."

Burton glanced over at Brownie as if surprised to see her hanging out with me. "Were you with Ann when she found Rufus?"

Brownie shook her head. "When I got there, she was giving Rufus CPR. I couldn't figure out what she was doing at first—it looked like she was attacking him or something. You know, it's dark back there because it's an alley."

Burton quirked an eyebrow as if having a tough time imagining a murderous librarian. To me he said, "Well, if he makes it, it's all due to you, Ann. That was good of you to check for a pulse and then spring into action like that."

"It's all that library training. We're supposed to be prepared for anything that could happen in the library because we're serving all sorts of age groups from all different walks of life. Brownie helped me out, too—she stepped in right before EMS got there. But Burton, his pulse was very faint. At first, I wasn't even sure he had one at all." I swallowed. "And that head injury seemed pretty bad to me."

"I'm going to check in over at the hospital as soon as I'm done here. Did either of you see anyone hanging around? Or anything suspicious? Any thoughts on what the weapon was?"

Brownie and I both shook our heads. Brownie said, "It must have been something heavy. I didn't see anything lying around back there."

"The perpetrator might have taken the weapon with him to dump later. Or maybe he dumped it back in the alley in one of the dumpsters back there." He focused on Brownie. "Any ideas who might have done this?"

"How would I know? I barely knew the guy . . . he was just somebody who served me coffee when I needed it."

I told myself that Brownie probably had no idea how pretentious she sounded. And that maybe she was still shaken up.

Burton said, "It was good you knew CPR. And sort of surprising, too . . . I wouldn't have thought that would be a skill you needed in your line of work."

Brownie shrugged. "I was a lifeguard every summer when I was a teen. I guess that sort of training just sticks with you. I kept up my certification, too. It's always a good public service reminder—I'd take pictures of my CPR card." She glanced over at me. "Ann was tired from giving it, so she asked me to step in." She paused. "Is he going to make it?"

Burton said grimly, "I'll be checking in with the hospital after I wrap up here. One more question for both of you: do you know of anyone who was upset enough with Rufus to do something like this?"

I shook my head. "I just engaged with small-talk with Rufus. He hasn't mentioned having an issue with anyone during our short conversations."

Brownie appeared to be considering the question carefully. She finally offered, "The only person I can imagine doing something like this is a disaffected employee. You read about those types of cases in the paper all the time, don't you? Somebody gets fired or doesn't think they've been treated fairly at work and the next thing you know, they go back to their workplace to get their revenge."

Burton frowned. "And you know one of these disaffected employees?"

"I wouldn't say I *know* her, any more than I knew Rufus. You know how it is when you come into a coffeehouse —you chat for a couple of minutes while they make your order. You talk about the weather or something like that. But I know Irene Bell worked here for a short period of time. You know she never stays somewhere long—that girl is plain restless. Anyway, she did very, very poorly over here."

Burton pulled out a tiny notebook and a stub of a pencil. "What kinds of things were going wrong?"

"Gracious; everything," said Brownie with a vehemence the situation didn't call for. "You could just tell this was the worst place in the world for her to work. She seemed positively frantic whenever I came in here. She spilled orders, she messed up orders. She *always* messed up my order."

I had to ask. "What's your usual order?"

"Cappuccino, no foam."

Of course it was.

Burton's brow furrowed. "All cappuccinos have foam."

Brownie gave him an annoyed look. "Not wet cappuccinos. They have more steamed milk."

It sounded to me like the kind of order a customer gave that was designed to make the barista panicky.

Burton was still mulling over the coffee order. "Why not just order a latte, then? A latte with no foam? That's basically what you're asking for."

Brownie gave a sniff that indicated she thought Burton was a total plebian.

Burton said, "So she wasn't a good barista."

"She was lousy at everything," snapped Brownie. "She got my change wrong on several occasions. I heard the other girl who worked here tell Irene she was late a few times, too. No wonder she can't ever keep a job. The point is that Rufus was unhappy with her, too, and fired her."

Burton tapped the stub of a pencil against the notepad. "And you think that made Irene angry enough to come back here and try to kill Rufus in an alleyway."

Brownie's neck and face grew splotchy with irritation. "How should I know? Like I said, I just share small talk with her from time to time. For all I know, she could be some sort of homicidal maniac who butchers everyone who stands in her way."

This mental image of Irene didn't quite square with the woman I saw in the pet store earlier.

Burton nodded. "Okay. Thanks for stepping in with the CPR. I think that's all I need from you."

Brownie looked around her. "What time do you think they'll be ready for business today?"

Burton raised his eyebrows and then said slowly, "I don't think I'd count on Keep Grounded opening up today. Better find your coffee elsewhere."

This statement didn't appear to improve Browne's mood. She slouched away, presumably to make coffee at home.

Burton watched her leave, shaking his head. "I wonder if she knows how awful she sounds?"

I chuckled. "Maybe it's just because she's got to put up such a happy, perfect face to the world as an online influencer. She can't hold up the act when she's not in front of a camera."

Burton glanced at his notes in the little notebook. "I'm not saying Irene isn't a suspect, but it just seems unlikely that she would come after Rufus because of revenge. Irene is fired just about every day of the week. She'd be out there murdering half the town."

His phone rang and he quickly took the call.

"I see. Yes. Thanks for the update." He hung up, looking somber. "Rufus didn't make it."

I felt myself slump and Burton quickly said, "Ann, there was nothing more that you or Brownie could have done to make sure Rufus made it."

I nodded, although I wasn't quite sure I believed him.

Burton must have seen I wasn't convinced because he added forcefully, "Look, the only person responsible for Rufus dying is the person who did this to him."

"Right. I'll keep my ears open and pass on whatever I hear." I paused. "What did you think about what Brownie said about Irene and Rufus?"

"I'd forgotten Irene worked here. It must not have been for very long." He shrugged. "From what I hear from her aunt, it's *never* very long. If she's a suspect, though, I guess it must have been fairly recently. Maybe right before she worked at the bank. I'll check into it. You're heading back to the library, right? Just want to make sure you're steady on your feet."

"I'm good, thanks. And definitely awake and alert now," I said wryly. "That was the whole reason I was over here to begin with—I needed caffeine to wake up. I'd better get back to work."

When I walked into the library, Wilson spotted me from his office and strode over.

"Ann? Are you okay?"

I nodded. "I'm fine. Unfortunately, Rufus didn't make it."

Wilson looked solemn. "I'm sorry to hear that. But it sounded like you did everything you could."

"The library's first aid training came in handy," I said with a short laugh. "I did call 911 to report what happened. They helped walk me through CPR because I was so keyed up, I wanted to make sure I did everything right."

"And so you did. You reflect well on the library, Ann."

It was high praise from Wilson. He gruffly continued, "You didn't mention on the phone how he'd sustained his injuries. Was he mugged, then? Was the coffeehouse robbed?"

I shook my head slowly. "It didn't appear that way. But he was definitely attacked—he had quite a head wound. The weapon wasn't obvious so I think Burton's team is going to have to hunt around for it."

Wilson frowned. "I just can't understand it. This happened in Whitby? In broad daylight? In the coffeehouse?"

"Not in the coffeehouse—behind it, in the alley. I went back there when no one came out to take my order in the shop. That's where I found Rufus."

Wilson said, "I see. I'm sure that was a startling thing to come across. You didn't see the perpetrator lurking around anywhere?"

"There was no one there at all."

Wilson said, "What a terrible experience. Don't you want to head home for the rest of day? You and Fitz?"

Fitz lifted his head at the sound of his name and gave a feline smile and purr. Wilson reached out absently to rub him.

I shook my head. "I'm fine. It's probably good for me to just stay busy today and this is the best place to do that."

"Well, at the least, take another break. It's not too busy here today and we have plenty of staff to cover things. I'm taking off a little early myself this evening."

I raised my eyebrows in surprise. Wilson was always someone who lived by the clock and any deviation from his schedule was rather astonishing. "Are you?"

A look of pride crossed his features. "I'm cooking a meal for Mona tonight. We're having a big day today—we went out together for lunch and are eating together tonight, too."

The news that he was cooking for Mona was even more mind-boggling than Wilson leaving the library early. "That's great, Wilson," I said, seemingly unable to access the rest of my vocabulary.

He nodded. "She's always cooking for me and bringing in snacks and food to the library. For all of us, really."

It was true. Mona was an excellent cook and she enjoyed cooking for others. She'd send in delicious quiches with Luna to the library, or bake coffee cakes or muffins for us. We'd all enjoyed the fruits of her labors.

Wilson continued, "I thought it would be nice to reciprocate. I've been planning out the meal I'm preparing and have all of the ingredients ready at home to jump in."

I had no doubt that Wilson was well-prepared. He was the sort of person who'd prepare for any exigency. But was he used to cooking? That was the million-dollar question. As far as I was aware, Wilson's nightly meals consisted of whatever the grocery store deli had in their prepared-foods area.

"What are you making?" I asked.

"I thought I'd do a pot roast," said Wilson. "I remember Mona saying it was one of her favorite comfort foods growing up."

From what I remembered about pot roast, it was also a rather tough cut of meat that needed time to make it tender. "Doesn't that take a while to cook?"

Wilson looked uncertain. "Well, I'm leaving work early, so it should be well in hand."

I didn't know much about cooking and Wilson looked so concerned that I quickly said, "I'm sure it will be great. And it's very thoughtful of you to cook for Mona. I'm sure she's going to love it."

He looked a bit more chipper. "Mona said she wasn't able to eat a lot of meat anymore because of Luna. I thought it might be a nice treat."

Luna was vegan and I'm sure the household likely didn't have a lot of meat-centered meals.

"Anyway, Ann, be sure to take some time off this afternoon."

I said, "Actually, I might head over to Grayson's house to check on him briefly. He's sick today."

"No worries. Like I said, we're fully-staffed today. Or, really, *over*-staffed." Wilson headed off cheerfully to work in his office and I worked on the bingo cards until it was break time. I decided my break would best be spent checking on Grayson so I headed over to his house.

Chapter Twelve

When I arrived, I was relieved to see Abby's car wasn't there. I told myself I was being pretty uncharitable to Abby—she'd probably just been over to check on her boss, like she'd said. Since she wasn't at his house now, she clearly wasn't totally camping out there, trying to make inroads on a relationship with him.

Grayson and I did have keys to each other's houses, a relatively new development. I decided this was a good opportunity to use mine, in case he was still sleeping. I walked into his house, which was usually full of sunlight, but which was now very dim with all the curtains pulled because of his migraine.

Grayson was on the sofa and had clearly been asleep until I opened the door.

"Sorry to wake you," I said softly. "I wanted to pop in and check on you to see how you were holding up."

He grimaced. "Not great. I forgot to mention when we were making disclosures about ourselves that I'm a terrible patient. I absolutely hate being sick."

"Not a problem," I said with a grin. "I'm not a great patient, myself. Can I get you anything? Something to drink? Do you want to take a stab at something to eat?"

He turned a little green at the mention of food. "I'll pass on food, for sure. And Abby already set me up with water." He gestured to a tremendous thermos that had Abby's name written on it. I was sure Abby would be delighted to return for it at a later time and then told myself I was being uncharitable yet again.

Grayson said, "It's more than just a migraine—it's some kind of virus. That's why I sent Abby away and why you need to head on out, too. I don't want you to catch anything from me."

I didn't want to catch anything, either. I'd been very truthful about being a bad patient. But he looked so pitiful and generally woebegone that I said, "How about if I drive you over to the doctor really quick and let them have a look at you? Maybe there's something they can do to make you feel better."

Grayson shook his head sorrowfully. "I've already called them. There's something going around and my symptoms were familiar to them. They said it was viral and I just needed to rest, stay hydrated, and basically wait it out."

"Is there anything I can take care of for you, then? Any errands you need running? I could go to the store for you."

Grayson raised his eyebrows. "Is Wilson just being supergenerous with your break today? I thought he was always snippy about people being punctual."

"Oh, he is snippy about it. But I've had a very unusual day so far," I said dryly. "Wilson has already informed me that I can have the rest of the day off if I want."

Grayson's eyebrows somehow managed to rise even higher. "That sounds like a story. Sit way over there and tell me about it."

So I sat across the room, projected my voice, and told him all about finding Rufus, Brownie's appearance in the alley, and Rufus's eventual demise. He listened, eyes narrowed.

"I'm sorry, Ann. That sounds awful."

I felt tears rise to my eyes and quickly blinked them away. "I just felt like there was something else I could have done to change the outcome."

Grayson was already shaking his head before I even finished the sentence. "It sounds like he wasn't going to make it no matter what. You could have been a trauma surgeon and the outcome still would have been the same."

"Burton did say something similar," I said.

"I wish I could give you a hug," he said sadly. "But I don't think we should risk it." He frowned. "Esther's funeral is tomorrow and I was planning on attending and seeing if I could pick up any additional information for the story I'm writing. There's obviously no way I'm making it, though. I'll have to get Abby to go in my place."

Over my dead body. "I can go for you. I'll jot down any notes about Esther and see if there's anyone I can speak with who might shed some light on these murders. That's what you're looking for, right? Tidbits about Esther for the profile and then information for the news story regarding the deaths."

He nodded and then winced as the movement apparently made his headache worse. He put a hand to his forehead and gently rubbed it. "That's right. Do you mind?" He frowned again. "Just be careful how much you push to find out information. With three mysterious deaths, somebody is obviously feeling desperate."

"I'll be careful. I like to think I just come off as curious. After all, I'm a research librarian so that sort of goes with the territory."

I noticed that Grayson's eyes were drooping and that his hand was now rubbing his eyes instead of his forehead.

"I'd better head on back to the library," I said. "I'll have my phone nearby, so just let me know if there's anything I can do to help you out."

He gave me a warm smile. "Thanks for checking on me."

"Maybe you should climb back into bed. Especially if your head is still hurting."

He gave me a rueful look. "Is it that obvious?"

I nodded with a smile. "A nap might make a big difference."

When I left, he was stumbling off in the direction of his bedroom.

The rest of the day at the library went well. When Fitz and I finally went home at the end of the day and I fell into blissful sleep with the orange cat curled up against my side as if we were a pair of spoons.

The next morning, I woke up early and checked on Grayson by email, since I didn't want to wake him if he was sleeping peacefully. He emailed me back immediately, assuring me that he sadly, *hadn't* slept peacefully and was heading to the doctor despite the fact that it seemed to be the virus du jour.

Fortunately, I was off from work so making it to Esther's funeral was no problem at all with my schedule. I dressed in something suitably somber and headed out the door.

The service was at the Presbyterian church instead of a graveside service. As I walked into the church, I could tell right away that Freddie had gone all-out for his mother's funeral. There were flowers everywhere, expensive-looking programs, and what looked like a full choir and a string quartet.

Sadly, although everyone in town must have recognized Esther because of her time in the square, attendance was sparse. Grayson's newspaper profile on her was going to be a good thing, I decided. It was a pity it didn't publish in time for the service. I did see Cora White in a pew and Zelda sitting grimly nearby. Cora looked very upset and was clutching a handful of used tissues. I remembered Cora blamed Zelda for stealing Esther's friendship away from her. From what I could tell, Cora was sitting ramrod straight in the pew and was studiously not looking in Zelda's direction.

The choir started up to indicate the service had begun. The minister delivered a message that was a bit of a sermon in length. Then Freddie rose to deliver the eulogy. The eulogy, though, didn't seem to have a lot to do with his mother—it had more to do with Freddie. It all seemed very much in character, however.

I did hear Freddie mention Esther more personally in one part of his eulogy, although he still managed to insert himself in the story. He talked about being a little kid and swiping some candy from the grocery store when his mother's back was turned. When they returned home and she discovered what he'd done, she'd marched him right back to the store and made him return it. What was more, she had him sweep the store for the manager, in penance for his deed. Freddie chuckled. "I never took anything from the store again."

There was a tittering laugh from the group. The laughter encouraged Freddie to continue.

"Yep, that was my mother. She was the kind of person who would carefully count her change at the store and if you gave her a penny too much, she'd immediately return it. Said she wanted to make sure the check-out clerk's cash drawer would balance at the end of the shift. Nice of her, but you'd never want to get behind her at the store. It took forever."

Everyone laughed again. I laughed too, but it made me think. If Esther was such an ethically-minded person, how seriously had she treated Irene's shoplifting? What if she'd noticed her taking something from the store and confronted her about it?

The service drew to a close after about an hour and we adjourned to the church hall for the reception. The hall was also covered with flowers—Freddie had clearly spared no expense. There was a hot buffet set up with what looked like far too much food for the number of people in attendance. I helped myself to some fried chicken, mashed potatoes and gravy, and green beans and sat down a bit closer to everyone than I liked, cognizant that I needed to try to gather information on Grayson's behalf.

I'd just started eating when Cora White sat down next to me. Her eyes were red from weeping. "May I sit with you, Ann?"

I nodded, washing down a bite of food with my water. "Of course. How are you doing?"

Unfortunately, my question made her immediately break down again. She swabbed at her face with the same handful of tissues I'd seen her with earlier and I scrabbled in my purse for a fresh pack, which I handed to her.

Cora gave me a grateful look. "Thank you."

A few minutes later, she took a shaky breath. "There. I think I'm better now. What a terrible week it's been."

I said gently, "It can't be easy to lose such a good friend."

Cora shook her head. "It's been just awful. Of course it would have been bad anyway, but it's even worse because Esther died before she and I could reconcile. Like I told you before, we'd known each other for nearly our entire lives. I can't believe she passed away during a rough patch in our friendship."

Just then, the alleged reason for the fracture in their friendship sat down with us. Zelda quirked an eyebrow. "Telling tales again, Cora?"

Cora shot her a look. "Only the truth, Zelda."

"Which is?" Zelda, whose plate had the distinction of being full of raw vegetables and fruits, paused to listen intently to Cora.

"That you stole Esther away from me," said Cora indignantly, a pink flush blooming up from her neck.

Zelda shook her head. "That's not the truth. The truth is that you weren't the best of friends to Esther. She decided she needed a friendship that wasn't toxic so she and I started hanging out with each other. End of story."

Zelda glanced across the room and raised her eyebrow again. "Need to talk to him," she said grimly.

We watched as she headed toward an innocuous-looking man who seemed unnerved at her approach. Most likely, he had committed some sort of homeowner association violation that Zelda was about to inform him of.

Cora was still bristling with annoyance. "Zelda is completely wrong. She's the one who persuaded Esther that our friendship wasn't working out. Can you imagine? A lifelong friendship not working out?" She gave a trembling sigh. "I just can't believe this week."

I gave her a sympathetic look, hoping it would spur her on as I continued eating my fried chicken plate.

Cora took my look as encouragement. "Rufus dying is horrible too, isn't it? I can hardly even take it in. Last night, I slept with my doors bolted and a chair under the door handle. It's absolutely terrifying." She frowned. "Did I hear that you were the one who discovered his body?"

I swallowed. "I did find Rufus, yes. He was still breathing at the time but he died shortly afterward."

She gave me a sympathetic look. "Gracious. I'm so sorry. I honestly don't know what this town is coming to. Burton seemed to think all three deaths are somehow connected: Esther's, Greta's, and Rufus's. He was asking me questions about Rufus."

"Did you know Rufus?" I asked.

"Not a bit," she said quickly. She glanced across the room to ensure Zelda was still chatting with the increasingly anxious-looking man. "Of course I knew he worked at the coffeehouse. I didn't even realize he was the owner until someone mentioned it to me."

I said, "I'm sure Burton is just trying to do his job and find out what happened."

Cora nodded miserably. "It's all just awful. Of course I feel bad for Greta and this Rufus, too. But I'm especially upset about Esther. She and I were on the verge of making up after our little spat. She'd smiled at me and given me a wave just the day before she died."

There was a derisive snort behind us and Cora whirled to see Zelda standing there with her hands on her hips. "What kind of nonsense are you spewing now, Cora? If Esther was smiling and waving, she was doing it at someone else. She was *not* about to make up with you. In fact, she was very upset that you were pestering her to death to be friends again."

Cora burst into tears, making me shift uncomfortably in my seat and push the tissue packet closer to her. Crying at a funeral isn't exactly unheard of, but glancing around, I could see most of the tables around us were looking in Cora's direction. Zelda wasn't wonderful at doing anything discreetly.

To her credit, Zelda looked a bit taken aback. She blinked a few times and then slowly sat in the chair next to Cora's. She awkwardly took her hand and patted it before Cora yanked it away from her. I couldn't blame Cora. Zelda hadn't exactly been making friendly overtures.

Zelda said gruffly, "You'll be all right. Just hang in there."

Cora wailed, "I'm just alone right now. Totally alone. Esther was the one person I counted on to hang out with me . . . pretty much my whole life. We went to movies or for walks in the park. Sometimes we just sat around and watched game shows together. I was good at Jeopardy! And she was better at Wheel of Fortune. Now I don't have anyone left."

Zelda looked rather appalled by this pronouncement. "You have your daughter, don't you? Dot or something?"

"Debra," said Cora with a sniff. "And, no, I don't have her, either. Debra's estranged herself from me."

This statement made more tears come to Cora's eyes. I quickly said, "Does she live here? Debra?"

Cora shook her head. "She moved away from Whitby fairly recently. She thought I was trying to interfere too much in her life, but I just wanted her life to be *wonderful* for her." She drooped in her chair. In a low, defeated voice she said to Zelda, "I know I was pestering Esther. She didn't mind being alone as much as I do. Esther was perfectly happy sitting in the square all day long, watching the birds and listening to people talk. I start getting antsy when I'm by myself."

Zelda was looking at Cora thoughtfully as if thinking she'd underestimated her. I wondered if Cora, with Esther gone, might now be considered possible friend material.

Cora rubbed her eyes, which only succeeded in making them look much worse. "I just keep wondering who could have done this to Esther. Who could have wanted to get rid of her?"

Zelda's lips tightened into a thin line, but she didn't say anything. It was clear she thought Cora was excellent suspect material.

"Are you coming up with any possible names?" I asked. "Is there someone who you know who was that upset with Esther?"

Cora shifted uncomfortably. "I hate to say anybody is capable of murder. That sounds like slander."

Zelda snorted. "You're not exactly making posters of the suspects and hanging them around town. You're just expressing your opinion."

"I guess. Well, I was thinking about Brownie and Lyle at first, you know. They simply couldn't stand Esther, could they? Lyle drove Esther crazy with his loud music, and she was never one not to express her opinion. Brownie seems to think her son can do no wrong, so she was angry and defensive with Esther for complaining about Lyle."

"But now you think it's someone else?" I asked.

She nodded. "What if it's Irene?"

Chapter Thirteen

Zelda frowned, eyebrows drawing together ferociously. "Who?"

"Irene Bell. A young woman about Ann's age. You know—she's worked everywhere in town and gotten fired from everywhere," said Cora.

Zelda still frowned so Cora elaborated, "Mary Schubert's niece."

"Oh, the ward," said Zelda, bobbing her head.

I didn't think I'd heard the word *ward* since I'd listened to Jane Austen audiobooks.

Zelda continued, "Why would Irene Bell have wanted to murder Esther? And Greta and Rufus? That all seems totally wrong."

"Well, you know," said Cora in a whisper that made Zelda and me lean in to hear her, "Esther saw the girl shoplifting. Esther was right there in the square, just hanging out like she always did, when she looked over and saw Irene take a packet of women's razors out from inside her jacket. She'd stolen them."

I wondered if it was a financial reason that made Irene decide to break the law. Women's razors were horribly expensive. Or was it more a sport for her? I'd gotten the impression that Mrs. Schubert would have forked over money for just about anything Irene needed.

Zelda shrugged. "So you think Irene murdered Esther because she spotted her shoplifting?"

Cora looked alarmed at the volume of Zelda's voice and quickly glanced around to ensure no one was listening to them.

Fortunately, everyone seemed ensconced in their own conversations.

"You don't think that's a good motive?" I asked.

Zelda shrugged again. "I'm just saying I don't think Irene was real motivated by the prospect of messing her life up if she was constantly getting fired. It doesn't sound like she was this perfect person who would have had her whole life come crashing down if she was exposed for being a shoplifter."

I considered this. "But maybe the shop would have called the police. Maybe she'd have been prosecuted and gone to jail. That might have been the final straw for Mrs. Schubert, causing her to wash her hands of her."

Zelda said with irritation, "Why is that young woman behaving that way to begin with? It sounds like her aunt has done everything possible to make sure she's taken care of."

Cora again lowered her voice, carefully looking around for eavesdroppers. "Well, she's had something of a rough life, you know. When she was little, she had a single mother."

I vaguely remembered that . . . Irene coming in for parent night with her one parent. I, of course, had no parents at all. I remembered it was something we had in common.

"Her mother tried her best, of course, but the fact of the matter is that Irene had very little supervision because her poor mother was working all the time to support her. Mary Schubert helped out when she could but Irene was always something of a handful. Then her mother got cancer. Really *bad* cancer and by the time she found out, it was already too late to do anything about it."

Zelda said in her grating voice, "So her aunt took her in."

Cora nodded. "And Irene did make life difficult for her. Mary had to deal with a teenager who wasn't motivated and was trying to process her mom's death. Plus, Irene was always asking for more."

Zelda nodded.

Cora took a deep sigh and looked at her nearly-full plate. "I'm not a bit hungry and being here is making me feel sad. I'm going to head out."

I quickly said, "Are you okay to drive? I know it's been an emotional day. I could wrap up my plate and take you back if you need a ride."

She shook her head with a small smile. "I'll be okay."

After she'd walked away, I gave Zelda a reproachful look. "You were kind of hard on her, don't you think?"

"I know, I know," she grouched. "But I can't tolerate lying and Cora was doing a lot of it. She acts like she was on the brink of making up with Esther and that couldn't be further from the truth." Zelda looked longingly outside. "I could use a cigarette."

I said, "Well, she's certainly broken up over Esther's death."

Zelda pressed her lips together. "Maybe she feels bad about bothering her to bits right before her death. She'd call her phone just about every hour, asking her to go with her to meals or see a movie or visit a friend. It was driving Esther batty."

For some reason, I never even thought about Esther carrying a cell phone. It seemed like a very modern device for someone who liked living a simple life.

"It sounded like Cora realized she was being pushy. Like she said, some people have a tough time being alone."

Zelda snorted. "She should have learned her lesson about being pushy with people. The same thing happened to her daughter. Esther told me about it. You know the man who just died? The coffeehouse owner?"

I frowned, feeling a sense of unease. "Rufus? Cora knew Rufus?" Cora had just finished telling me that she had *not* known him.

"That's the one," said Zelda crisply. "Cora's daughter was involved with him and Cora didn't like it. For some reason, she'd taken an instant dislike to Rufus. Cora tried to interfere in the situation and irritated Rufus so much that he ended up breaking off the relationship with her."

I raised my eyebrows. "And her daughter ended up leaving town."

"Fed up with her mother trying to manage her life," said Zelda with a sniff.

"That must have made Cora feel terrible," I said slowly.

Zelda shrugged her thin shoulders. "Maybe it did. She obviously feels bad about it now. But at the time, she just said it was right for a mother to be protective." She glanced across the room and I followed her gaze to see Freddie Jenkins, who'd been boisterously greeting everyone at each table, heading in our direction.

"Gotta get out of here," muttered Zelda. "Don't like that guy."

She somehow managed to finish off her plate and slink away before Freddie joined us.

Freddie sat down across from me and beamed at me. "Good to see you here. Hey, I wanted you to tell your guy that if he needs more info for the story on Mama, that I've got plenty."

It seemed to me that Freddie might have been drinking before the service. Or possibly before the reception . . . or both. I wondered if he carried a flask with him. His face was flushed, his eyes very bright, and his words just a bit slurred. He was in quite a jolly mood, despite the grim occasion.

Maybe I looked a little surprised because Freddie said, "Isn't this great? It's just what Mama would have wanted."

But, reflecting back on Esther's introversion and the way she stayed in the background, I didn't think that necessarily was the case.

Freddie said, "Mama did lead a good, long life. It wasn't her time to go and *that* makes me feel angry. But I'm not as angry as I would have been if her life had been *really* cut short. Like the coffeehouse guy."

"Rufus."

"Yeah, that's right. A terrible thing."

I was just starting to feel like Freddie was actually going to show some sympathy for another person when I realized exactly what the "terrible thing" was as he continued.

"I mean, what are we going to do about getting coffee now? There's no decent coffee anywhere else in Whitby. It's gross over at Quittin' Time."

I said in a slightly cooler tone than I'd intended, "I guess there's always home brew."

Freddie shook his head. "Just not the same. I want to go after the people who killed Rufus because they didn't think things through. They basically shot themselves in the foot."

Freddie seemed, again, to mostly consider events as they affected him. "Did you know Rufus, then?"

"Only from getting coffee in there. So, not really."

I spotted Zelda coming back into the church hall and frowned, wondering why she'd returned.

Freddie was continuing, "Anyway, I appreciate you being here today."

"I'm so sorry about Esther. I've enjoyed learning more about her with the piece Grayson is preparing for the paper."

Freddie said with a sigh, "Yeah, I miss her. We both got along great, you know. We were real close."

Zelda arrived at our table in enough time to overhear Freddie. She snarled, "That's funny. I never saw you and Esther together."

Freddie looked momentarily startled. Then he gave a half-hearted laugh. "You've forgotten, then."

Zelda's eyes narrowed. She clearly didn't like having her memory disparaged in such a way. "Oh, I don't forget things. Esther told me that you only visited her when you needed money."

Freddie gave a rumbling chuckle. "Well, it so happened that I needed money pretty frequently. I saw Mama plenty."

Zelda snorted, reached down to retrieve her forgotten cell phone from her chair, and stomped out the door.

"Temperamental, isn't she?" asked Freddie.

I smiled. "Yes."

Freddie said, "Well, thanks for coming to Mama's shindig. I hope she's smiling down at us today. And that she's happy."

"I'm sure she is."

Freddie continued, "She wasn't one to indulge herself, you know? She'd never have thrown a party like this for her own benefit. And I told you how frugal she was—she never did much for herself. I'm not even sure she was all that happy. If she'd left town more than she did, I bet she'd have had a better life."

I thought this was probably Freddie projecting. *He* clearly was interested in travel. But Esther had always seemed perfectly content when I'd seen her out in the square. She never appeared to be nodding off; she was always attentive—engaged with her surroundings and the people around her. I never saw her looking bored or unhappy. There was one other thing that I remembered, too.

I said, "I was thinking Cora had mentioned to me that Esther liked travelling and that Zelda and your mother would go on day trips from time to time."

Freddie made a face. "Going on a day trip isn't exactly what I had in mind. I was thinking more like a cruise or a European vacation. Maybe if she'd traveled, she'd have been more . . . I don't know . . . fulfilled. She burned through a lot of time just watching people walk by."

I said, "I wouldn't feel too bad about that. She clearly had the funds to travel and seemed to be in good health. If she'd wanted to see the world, she probably would have."

Freddie brightened at this and I realized that maybe he really did feel bad for the insular life his mother led. "True. Well, maybe I'll see the world on her behalf. I've always wanted to."

"Where are you thinking about going?"

A dreamy look settled over Freddie's features. "Europe first. Paris, Rome. Oh, and I'd love to go to New Zealand, too. I'm going to sit down and approach it from a real organized way—make a list of all the places I want to go and put them in order."

"That sounds like a smart plan," I said. "We've got plenty of travel books at the library, too, if you want to check them out. They might be able to give you some direction."

Freddie looked interested. "You know, I totally forgot about the library. Good point. That'll save me having to buy travel guides." He looked thoughtful. "Maybe I should bone up on home renovations, too. It would sure make the place easier to unload."

"Are you thinking of selling your mom's place?" This was surprising, since the last time I'd spoken with him, he was planning on moving in.

"Yeah. I was moving my stuff in and realized that I'd rather start from scratch, you know? Too many memories of my mom there. Anyway, I'll stay there while I fix the place up. Then I'll put it on the market and use some of the money to fund my travel and whatnot."

I said, "The next-door neighbors seemed interested in your mother's property."

Freddie's eyebrows shot up. "Were they? I mean, I know they used to be and Mama wouldn't even listen to them. I kept telling her she should sell to them. But they still might want it?"

"It might be worth stopping by and finding out," I said.

Freddie beamed. "Then I wouldn't have to even do anything to the house at all. Not if they're going to knock it down anyway and just use the property. That'll make life easier."

He glanced around the room then as if he was hosting a party instead of a funeral reception. And maybe he was. I said, "This is more of a celebration of life reception, isn't it? I think you've done a great job with it."

The praise pleased Freddie. "Exactly. I didn't want anyone to be here with long faces. I'd even wanted to have an open bar but the church nixed that. I guess they don't allow alcohol in the church hall or something. But the food has been good and most people seem like they're having a good time. It's better to just think about Mama and what a great gal she was and not be sad." He frowned. "Except for Cora. Was she okay? I saw her break down a couple of times. I know she grew up with Mama and was a good friend of hers. At least, until recently."

I nodded. "She was feeling sad and thought it would be better if she headed off home."

Freddie snorted. "Maybe she was feeling guilty and that made her sad."

"Guilty?" I asked.

Freddie said, "Sure. She'd been bugging Mama to death lately. Trying to stick to her like glue. Or maybe she feels guilty because she had something to do with Mama's death."

"What makes you think she might have?"

Freddie said, "Well, because she was mad at Mama. Let's face it—she was furious about being alone. My mother was her only real friend, especially since Cora's daughter left town. I guess you know the reason for that?" He lifted up an eyebrow.

I nodded. "Because Cora didn't like who she was dating."

"Right. And look who else is dead now! Rufus."

It still seemed something of a leap to me. But Freddie sounded very confident.

He must have been able to read the doubt on my face because he said, "Cora was with my mom when she fell *another* time. Mama was hanging out in the square like usual and Cora came up to talk to her about being friends again. Mama stood up to greet her and Cora gave her a shove."

"What? Does Burton know about this?"

Freddie nodded smugly at my reaction. "Sure, he does. I told him if it had happened once, it could happen again. Cora could have lashed out at my mother again, pushed her, and then Mama fell back and hit the back of her head."

I said, "And your mother filled you in about it? The first time, I mean?"

Here Freddie looked a little sketchy. "Well, she was trying to protect Cora, you know. That's the way she was. She told me she'd lost her balance when she stood up to greet Cora in the square. But I saw her face and the way she wouldn't meet my eyes. She was covering up what happened so Cora wouldn't look like the bad guy."

Freddie glanced around the room again, suddenly looking restless. "Well, I gotta go talk to some of the other guests. Thanks for coming, Ann."

He'd called all the mourners "guests." Again, I got the impression that Freddie felt as if he was hosting a big party. But then, if it really was a celebration of life, maybe that's how it should be. Having spoken with Freddie, I decided to slip out.

Chapter Fourteen

I called Grayson from my car. "Are you hanging in there?"

Grayson sounded sort of pitiful, which made me think he was probably feeling better. Before, he'd felt too sick to feel sorry for himself. "I'm trying," he said bravely.

"Would a visit from Fitz make you feel any better? He's practically a therapy animal from all his time cuddling patrons in the library."

Grayson's voice sounded a lot more upbeat now. "A visit from you and Fitz would make me feel *much* better. But make sure you keep your distance; I don't want to pass this along to you."

I stopped by the house to get Fitz and my cat carrier. Fitz was just waking up from a nap and stretching in a kitchen sunbeam, an alert look on his furry face.

"Ready to do some visiting?" I asked.

He must have been sleeping for most of the time I was gone because he was wide-eyed and bushy tailed. He trotted right into the cat carrier and proceeded to groom himself in there for whatever visit might be forthcoming. When we got to Grayson's, I opened the door and set the carrier down.

Fitz came out a bit cautiously, uncertain of the new environment, but with his tail held high. Once he spotted Grayson, he gave a little chirp and bounded over to see him.

Grayson rubbed Fitz and the cat bumped his head gently against Grayson's. "Hey, buddy," he said softly. "Thanks for coming over to help me feel better."

"How are you feeling? And what did the doctor say?"

Grayson gave me a wry look. "Unfortunately, it's a virus, so I do just have to wait it out. But I'm already feeling a bit better. I appreciate your coming by. And thanks for going to Esther's funeral. How did everything go?"

I said, "Well, I'm not sure that I got more human-interest story info. Freddie gave Esther's eulogy."

Grayson chuckled. "Let me guess—the eulogy was all about Freddie."

"I guess he tied it in with his mother from time to time. Sort of." I smiled back at him. "But he definitely didn't share anything that we didn't already know. I did see Cora there, though, and had the chance to talk with her."

"I'm guessing Zelda was at the service, too," said Grayson.

I made a face. "She was. And she had Cora in tears, not that Cora wasn't *already* in tears."

"Zelda's nearly had *me* in tears before, so I can totally see that. What did she say to her?"

I said, "Oh, she was contradicting something Cora said. Cora told me that she and Esther had been on the point of making up again but Zelda said that wasn't at all true. In Zelda's eyes, Cora had been basically stalking Esther, trying to force her back into their friendship."

Grayson raised an eyebrow. "I'm guessing that wasn't particularly effective."

"No. But Cora gave a little background that might explain why she was being so persistent—she said that she was totally alone now. Her daughter apparently also felt Cora was a little too pushy, and she moved away to live her life elsewhere."

Grayson winced. "That must have been rough for Cora."

"It seemed to be. But the big reveal of the day was that Cora knew Rufus, despite saying she didn't. Her daughter had been dating him, Cora had disapproved, and that's what had prompted her daughter to move away."

Grayson frowned. "How did you find out Cora did know Rufus?"

"Courtesy of Zelda, who apparently knows all. Clearly, Zelda thinks Cora makes for a very good suspect."

Grayson didn't seem to be quite as convinced as Zelda was. "I can sort of see her accidentally killing Esther—maybe she shoved her out of frustration and then she was shocked by the outcome. But I have a hard time believing she'd kill Rufus because her daughter used to date him at one point."

"Maybe she killed him because he knew something. The coffeehouse is right there on the square, after all. Rufus could have stepped out of the shop for a second and seen something," I offered.

Grayson said, "That makes sense. The only problem is—why *didn't* Rufus say anything to the cops? Esther's death was considered an accident until Greta died after saying she'd seen something suspicious."

I said slowly, "Could Rufus have considered blackmailing Cora? I'm sure Cora would be desperate to keep out of prison."

"Could be," said Grayson thoughtfully.

After a pause, I said, "There was one more reason Cora might be the one who killed Esther. When I spoke with Freddie, he said this had happened before—that Cora had been with Esther on an earlier occasion and pushed Esther out of frustration.

Esther had fallen and gotten banged up from the fall. It seems Esther didn't have very good balance."

"I'm sure that incident didn't help convince Esther that she needed to resume her friendship with Cora," said Grayson dryly.

"Probably not." I thought back to the funeral service and said, "I didn't find out very much more from Freddie. He did say that he was planning on selling Esther's house."

"That was a quick change of mind, considering he was planning on moving in."

I said, "I got the impression that he wants something a little grander. He was going to fix up her house, but I mentioned that the neighbors seemed to still be interested in buying the property."

Grayson chuckled. "That must have cheered him up—not having to do any renovations to the house."

"Exactly."

Grayson said, "Well, Freddie's motive has always been very plain—money. Although I'm not totally sure I can see him shoving his mother in public. That doesn't seem like something he'd do."

"He does seem like he'd be more of the type of person to do something scurrilous in private, doesn't he?"

"Poison or an accident at home," agreed Grayson, looking just a bit sleepy.

I stood up and said, "Time for me to leave you alone so you can get a nap in. Is there anything I can get for you before I go?"

He shook his head, closing his eyes. "No thanks, Ann."

I extricated Fitz from him and headed back home to spend the rest of the day quietly with a book and a cat.

The next morning, I decided to start off my day being very wholesome. I was on the schedule to close up the library and my shift didn't start until noon, so I had plenty of time to exercise and hit the grocery store for some healthy items to take to the library for snacks and lunch. After feeding Fitz and giving him a little love, I drove the car downtown and walked from there to the park.

I was stretching near a park bench when I heard someone call my name. I looked up and saw Luna there.

"Want to join me?" I asked. I remembered Luna had the day off completely.

Luna gave me a skeptical look. "Are you running or walking?"

"I think it'll just be a brisk walk today."

Luna nodded. "Sure, I'll join you. Although I guess I'm really not dressed for it."

She was wearing a long skirt of many different colors and a bright lime-green top that probably wouldn't have suited many people, but looked great on Luna.

"You're pretty dressed up," I said slowly.

She nodded, not meeting my eyes. "Jeremy and I are going to lunch today. Baby steps, you know. Next time maybe it'll be supper."

I felt my heart sink a little bit as we started out on a walk.

Luna sighed. "Don't worry, Ann. I had a talk with Burton yesterday. I felt so, so awful about it."

I felt marginally better, although I still felt bad for Burton. "I'm glad you leveled with him."

Luna sighed again and this time the sigh sounded a little broken. "He looked so sad. I felt like the worst person ever."

This made me smile a little. "I'm pretty sure someone else holds the record for worst person ever."

"Maybe," said Luna doubtfully. "But still, I felt pretty rotten. I told him that I wanted to be honest with him and that I'd loved our time together. But that I didn't think we were right for each other. That he deserved someone who could be 100 percent devoted to him. And he does—he's amazing. He just wasn't right for me."

Luna had started walking faster as she talked and I was breathing a bit harder. "You did the right thing, Luna, being straight with him. I'm sure he appreciated that on some level, even though he was upset. He's the kind of guy who appreciates honesty."

"I guess you're right. I was just feeling so conflicted and horrible that I'm glad I finally broke things off. It's going to be so awkward the next time I see him, of course." Luna looked leery at the idea.

"Maybe. But it'll get better with time."

"I hope so. I felt guilty about breaking up with him right in the middle of this big case he's working. When I caught up with him yesterday, it looked like he hadn't even had any sleep the night before. Then I ended things and he looked even worse." Luna made a face.

I shook my head. "There would never have been a perfect time to break up with him, Luna. You absolutely did the right thing."

Luna grinned at me. "I almost forgot to tell you my good news because I've been so worried about Burton. Guess what?"

When someone said that to me, I always tried to take a stab at it. "You won the lottery." Luna was always one to pick up a ticket whenever she got gasoline.

She rolled her eyes at me. "As if! Do you think I'd be here right now? I'd be out on a beach somewhere with a server bringing me frozen drinks with little umbrellas in them. No, I got my proposal approved by Wilson!"

Luna held her hand up for a high-five and I gave it to her. "That's fantastic, Luna!"

She nodded, beaming. "Isn't it great? The teen yoga class is going ahead. I'll get to wear my yoga pants one day a week to work. And it's all due to you."

I shook my head. "You're the one who sold it to Wilson, Luna. You're the one with the great idea. I just showed you how to wrangle the red tape."

"Well, you know I'm never a huge fan of red tape. I practically break out into hives when I have to go to the Department of Motor Vehicles. There's something about all that monochrome coloring in the same place." Luna shivered and looked down at her wildly multicolored attire to soothe herself. "But writing a proposal for Wilson was obviously the way to go. I did just what you said—did some research and showed him some numbers about what other libraries were doing with their teen programs and what the engagement rate was."

"Congratulations, Luna. When does it start?"

Luna said, "I'm thinking a couple of weeks from now. That way I can plan the program and try to drum up attendance."

I nodded. "I can make flyers and try to recruit teens when they come to the circulation desk. And put it all over our social media, of course."

"That would be awesome, Ann. Oh, and can we have Fitz on the flyers?"

I chuckled. "Of *course* we can. It's not even considered a Whitby Library flyer if it doesn't have Fitz's face on it somewhere. He'll be delighted to promote the yoga class. If you bring in a yoga mat, I can take pictures of him on it. He's gotten great at posing."

Luna's eyes opened wide. "I just remembered—Wilson gave me a little bit of budget to buy yoga mats in case anyone shows up without one. I'll have to go pick those up. He actually gave me the library credit card and a budget. I'm going to see how far I can make the money go. When he handed that card to me it was as if the heavens opened up and angels were singing. I felt like a real, valued employee."

Luna was starting to sound pretty breathless as we practically sprinted down the park path. "Uh, you're right. I'm not dressed for this."

I smiled at her. "Yeah. You set the pace, though."

"Only because I was agitated from talking about this stuff," said Luna, gasping. "I'm out of here. Catch you later, Ann."

"Let me know how your lunch with Jeremy goes," I called after her. She waved a hand silently in response.

I resumed the fast pace which was a lot easier when I didn't have to engage in conversation and took in the beautiful surroundings. The park was my favorite place to exercise with a view of the mountains in the background, the small lake the path adjoined, and the dog-walkers along the way.

Plus, I loved starting out my day with exercise. It made me feel like I'd accomplished something major, right off the bat.

Afterwards, I decided to treat myself by running by the used bookstore. I loved popping by there sometimes—for one thing, it helped give me ideas for books for our library's acquisition. For another, sometimes I'd happen across unusual books that maybe weren't right for our catalog but were interesting for me to read.

I parked the car and headed down the sidewalk toward the bookshop. I passed the pet store along the way and saw Irene Bell standing outside looking at her phone. It seemed a little early for a break, but Irene looked very casual about it. She smiled at me when I approached.

"Hey there," she said. "How did the toy go over with Fitz?"

I grinned back at her. "Oh my gosh. He *loved* it. He was exhausted by the time he finished playing with that thing. He knew it wasn't alive, but he was having a great time *pretending* it was alive and attacking it."

Irene chuckled. "I bet. Another customer brought her cat in to try out some toys and the cat went absolutely wild."

"Exactly. I think it's the noises the toy makes. Sort of like a mouse or some other small rodent. It sounds like it's going through its death throes. Makes Fitz feel like a tough guy."

Irene said, "Aww! I'm going to have to run by the library on my day off just to see Fitz. I'm not much of a reader, but I'd love to visit your cat. As long as my aunt isn't there," she added with a grimace.

"He'd love to visit with you. And you should take a look around the library. I know you come by to get some of our movies sometimes. We have a lot more than just books over there. You can check out music, magazines, take classes—all kinds of stuff."

Irene looked a little surprised. "Really? I'll have to come by and take a look."

"I'd be happy to give you a little tour when you come. It's always good to know all our resources."

"I'll have to do that." She paused. "How have things been going? I know you're kind of plugged in to everything going on in town. Have you heard if the police are making any progress?"

I shook my head. "I'm afraid I don't know one way or another. But I don't think their investigation is close to wrapping up."

"No, I guess not, especially with another murder." Irene looked somber for a moment. "I heard about the coffeehouse owner. Not that I really knew him, of course, but word gets around."

Chapter Fifteen

Something in me decided not to let that pass. I said, "Oh, I was thinking your aunt told me you used to work there."

Irene's eyes flashed, either at the mention of her aunt or the fact that she'd been caught in a mistruth.

"I guess it would be more accurate for me to say that I didn't really know Rufus *now*. You're right—I did know him from the shop, but only from a work standpoint. He and I weren't friends or anything. Burton already hunted me down to find out the scoop about Rufus. Of course I didn't even have an alibi; I live totally by myself."

"Same," I said with a smile.

Irene relaxed her defensive posture a little. "If I had a more interesting life, I wouldn't be at home all the time and maybe I *would* actually have an alibi when something like this happened."

She made it sound as if needing an alibi were an everyday occurrence. A dreamy look came over Irene's features. "I could totally see myself on a Greek isle somewhere. Maybe in one of those whitewashed little villas that are always sun-dappled. Right by the bright blue sea." Then she sighed. "Instead, I'm stuck here in Whitby."

Of course, there were far worse places than Whitby to be stuck. Whitby had a lake, mountains, and gorgeous sunsets. People retired to the town monthly. But Irene was clearly in no frame of mind to hear me wax poetic about our hometown.

She shifted course. "And Whitby doesn't even seem all that safe right now. Obviously somebody wasn't very happy with Rufus. And the cops think it's connected to the old lady's death." She frowned. "And, of course, that *other* old lady, I guess."

Poor Greta's death always seemed to be eclipsed by the others. I nodded.

Irene shrugged. "I didn't know anything about the other lady they talked to me about when they came around again. Gretchen?"

"Greta," I said.

"Right. I'm not sure even what happened to her, but the cops acted like it was foul play. I didn't know anything about Esther, either, but I could totally see where she might get on somebody's bad side."

I just nodded, not saying anything, and hoping Irene would fill in the blanks.

Which she did. "Esther just sat around and watched *everybody* all the time. She was a huge snoop. I think she gossiped, too, spreading all kinds of misinformation around. You know, people don't *want* to have their private business aired out in public. Especially in a small town where everybody knows everyone else."

I asked, "Did she gossip about you, too?"

Irene pressed her lips together. "Who knows? Probably. Esther did know about a mistake I made and she wasn't going to leave me alone about it. Every time I saw her, her big eyes just stared at me, like she was trying to make me feel guilty or something. But we all make mistakes, don't we? I'm sure she made plenty of mistakes, herself. But most of the time other people don't know about them." She suddenly looked uneasy. "If you don't mind, keep that under your hat, will you? People won't understand and then they'll think I killed Esther to keep her quiet."

I wondered if Burton was included among the "people" who wouldn't understand. I nodded again. It also occurred to me that Irene had acted as if she hadn't known Esther at all the last time I spoke with her. Now she was able to espouse an opinion about how she might have irritated people around her.

Irene continued, "I don't think Rufus was all that easy to get along with, either. Maybe he pushed someone just a little too far and then they lashed out at him."

"Did he seem to have many friends?"

Irene shook her head. "Tons of acquaintances because of people coming into the shop for their caffeine fix. But he sort of kept to himself—as far as I could tell, anyway. Like I said, I didn't know him all that well. And that job didn't work out so I wasn't there for long."

If Irene *had* been fired from the coffeehouse gig, it didn't seem to have upset her that much. She was very casual about not working there long.

"How are things going at the pet store?"

Irene brightened a little. "It's pretty good. I think I've decided that I'm not a fan of working with humans, but working with dogs and cats is just fine."

I chuckled. "Yeah, animals can be a lot easier to deal with. They're not as complicated as people, anyway. Whenever I'm having a rough day at the library, I look over and see Fitz. It makes my blood pressure go down."

Irene mulled this over. "The only bad thing is that the dogs can't come into the shop on their own. They have people come in with them. It'd be great if dogs could do their own shopping and I wouldn't have to deal with their snippy owners all the time. I do like the times when it's just me and Bobo at the pet store. He sleeps most of the time, but he makes me feel relaxed by just being around."

"That's why Fitz works so well at the library. It's his personality and the way nothing fazes him."

We turned as a jaunty voice behind us said, "Coffee break?"

It was Freddie Jenkins beaming at us both.

Irene seemed both flustered and delighted to be addressed. "Something like that," she said breathlessly.

Freddie stuck out a hand. "Freddie Jenkins. I've seen you around town, but I don't think we've actually met."

Irene shook his hand, blushing a little. I blinked. This was a development that I hadn't seen coming.

"You work at the pet store?" asked Freddie curiously.

Irene nodded shyly. "I've been bouncing around a little from job to job, though, so you might have seen me somewhere else. Although I really do like this job—I was just telling Ann that."

Freddie says, "I'll have to come in and see what it's like in there. I've never been."

I said, "Do you have pets, Freddie?"

Freddie grinned at me. "I never had time before to keep up with them. But things are changing now. Maybe I should start slow and build my way up. I could get some fish or something."

Irene said hesitantly, "I'd be happy to show you what we've got, if you want to take a look."

"Why not?" said Freddie, grinning at her. "Sounds like the perfect way to start out my day."

Freddie and Irene walked into the shop together, Irene's face flushed with excitement and Freddie looking positively buoyant.

Hours later, I'd run all my errands, packed up Fitz, and was about to head into the library for my afternoon shift.

I glanced across the parking lot and saw my favorite patron, Linus, with his sweet dog, Ivy. He raised a hand in greeting and I walked over carrying Fitz in his carrier.

It's a testament to how chilled out Fitz was that he welcomed the sight of a large dog of indeterminate heritage. Ivy sniffed carefully near his carrier and Fitz rolled playfully onto his back.

Linus gently pulled Ivy back away from the carrier.

"I don't think Fitz minds," I said with a laugh.

"He's quite a cat," said Linus admiringly. "He's always so laid back—whenever I've seen him, anyway."

"You should see him with his new toy, though. He acts like it's his sworn duty to kill it. It makes me laugh."

Linus said thoughtfully, "You got it at the local pet shop? Or online?"

"I picked it up locally. They have tons of toys there if you're looking for something for Ivy."

Ivy perked up at her name and I leaned forward and scratched her behind her ears as she gave me an approving look, whether for the scratching or the mention of a toy, I wasn't sure.

Linus nodded. "That young woman works there, doesn't she? She's about your age."

"Irene Bell? Yes, she and I went to school together."

"You're friends?" Linus's forehead puckered worriedly.

I carefully said, "Not close friends, no. Is something wrong?"

Linus hesitated and then said in a rush, "I believe she used to work for the coffeehouse, didn't she? Or was it the bank?"

I gave him a wry smile. "I think it was both, actually. Irene doesn't seem to have a very good track record when it comes to sticking with jobs."

"You see . . . I saw her early in the morning when I was out walking Ivy. On the morning the coffeehouse owner, Rufus, died." He sighed. "I thought at the time she seemed as if she was acting a little suspicious. She was looking around furtively. I wondered—well, I wondered if she might have been up to no good."

"Where was she when you saw her?" I asked. Could she have been shoplifting at the coffeehouse and been caught by Rufus? Or at another nearby shop?

"She was coming out of the alleyway behind the coffeehouse. I didn't realize until just a little while ago when I was reading the paper where Rufus was found—and when. I thought at the time that maybe I was just getting to be paranoid about my safety." He sighed. "I'm not wanting to get anyone into trouble, especially if there's a perfectly reasonable explanation, but I was trying to figure out if I should tell Burton."

"Oh, I definitely think you should," I said quickly. "Leave it up to Burton to decide whether it's an important piece of information or not."

"There was something else, too," Linus said. "I was planning on speaking with Burton, but then Rufus died and I figured I must have been wrong."

"Wrong?"

He nodded. "Greta used to engage in some small talk with me. I thought she was a very nice woman and a good library volunteer. She was very particular about shelving books in the right place. She was a very slow, thoughtful worker."

Which, as I recall, used to drive Zelda crazy.

Linus continued, "She spotted my coffee cup from Keep Grounded one morning and frowned at it. She said she wasn't visiting the coffeehouse anymore because she'd seen Rufus being rough with Esther."

"Being rough?" I asked.

He nodded. "I didn't ask her to elaborate. I'd thought at the time that she might be referring to rough language or an ugly tone of voice or something. But later, I started wondering if Rufus had been responsible for Esther's death." He sighed. "It took me a while to catch on that Esther's death hadn't been accidental."

"Well, it took a while for the *police* to determine that, too. Everyone had assumed it was accidental. It was only after Greta's death that they even introduced that as a possibility."

Linus said slowly, "I wondered if Greta's death resulted from the fact that she was going around town talking about having seen something suspicious. Before I could speak to Burton about it, Rufus had been killed and so it appeared that my concern was unfounded. I never ended up speaking with him about it."

I considered this. "I wonder if Greta was telling a lot of people about having seen Esther being pushed around."

Linus nodded somberly. "Maybe the killer thought she was referring to him when she was actually thinking it was Rufus all the time. I'll call Burton up and tell him what she said. He's always so sensible that I'm sure he'll handle the information appropriately." He looked at his watch. "Heading into the library?"

I smiled at him. "I've got an afternoon shift today. I'll see you after you finish walking Ivy. If you're keeping to your usual schedule of course."

"Naturally, I am," he said with a smile of his own. "See you soon, then."

The library was a whirlwind of activity when I walked in there. The bingo cards were apparently a hit and I realized I needed to print out some more for the circulation and reference desks. It seemed to be taking off. It was even better that patrons were filling their bingo sheets and then uploading them online and tagging the library. I smiled at people who had the little pieces of paper in their hands and were checking out books that were outside their usual comfort zone or a book that was published the year they were born. Sometimes patrons came over to get some help with their sheet and I was happy to give them a hand and point them in the direction of some great titles that I thought might suck them in.

After I'd printed off more cards, I had a woman come over to me with her laptop.

"I'm sorry," she said. "I'd usually try to wait for one of your tech drop-ins, but I'm having a real computer emergency."

I recognized the middle-aged woman as someone who was a regular attendee at our tech drop-ins. Timothy, who was our youngest film club member, graciously helped out at the computers for volunteer hours for his college applications. This lady had myriad devices which she claimed were all on their last legs . . . although the issue was usually something that was easily fixed.

"No problem; I can help you out," I said. "What's going on with your laptop?"

"It's frozen," she said, staring grimly at it. "It won't move at all."

"Did you try to reboot it?" I asked.

The woman gave me a blank look.

"Restart it?" I clarified.

"I can't. It's frozen."

I carefully took the laptop from her and sat it in front of me on the reference desk. I moved my finger on the touchpad. The cursor on the screen moved along with me.

"It seems to be working fine, now," I said brightly.

The middle-aged woman gave me and the device a similarly suspicious look. "It couldn't be."

I turned the laptop around and then came around the desk to stand next to her. "Show me what you're doing that makes the computer frozen," I said.

She immediately put her finger on the laptop screen, moving it around. "See?" she asked in frustration. "Nothing moves."

I shook my head. "It's not a touchscreen laptop."

"What?"

"Touching the screen on this laptop won't do anything, unfortunately. You have to move the cursor with the touchpad at the bottom of the keyboard for this particular laptop." I showed her what I was talking about and her eyes opened wide.

Then she flushed. "I feel silly."

"Don't—every computer is different, right? This one just doesn't have the bells and whistles you're used to. And when you can't figure out how to move on the screen, it can be really frustrating."

She nodded and gave me a smile. "Thank you." Taking her computer, she walked back out of the library just as a young man slouched inside.

I realized the young man was Lyle, who didn't exactly look pleased to be at the library. He bobbed his head at me in greeting before heading over to the study area. I saw him look around for a moment, shrug, and head back over to me.

"Something wrong?" I asked.

"Tutor's not here," he said gruffly. "So I'm just going to head out."

I looked at my watch. "Looks like you're just a couple of minutes early if you're supposed to be meeting your tutor at the top of the hour. Can you wait a little while?"

He gave a sigh as if he was being extremely put-upon. "I guess so, yeah. I don't think I even need tutoring at all. It's my mom's idea. She wants me to be totally perfect like everything she posts online. Too bad I don't measure up."

I shook my head. "Your mom loves you, you know. From what I know about influencers, which isn't a lot, it's sort of part of the job to display a perfect life. Isn't it?"

He gave a short laugh. "Yeah. But usually the family doesn't fall as short of the mark as ours does. My dad is never around.

When he *is* in town, he's doing his best to stay away from us in his office. And my mom is obsessed with making our house even bigger than it already is so we can be even further away from each other." He shook his head and added bitterly, "Maybe my mom loves me, but she sure doesn't like me. If she did, she couldn't think I'm a killer."

Chapter Sixteen

"What?"

"That's right," he said in that same gruff voice, "my mother thinks I killed two old ladies and Rufus."

I said slowly, "What makes you think that?"

He shrugged. "She never trusts me. Mom always thinks I'm up to no good or falling down on the job. The 'job' is to be the perfect son who always combs his hair, wears dressy clothes, and makes great grades. She thinks I'm actually a total mess."

I could see through Lyle's tough exterior that he was really hurt and confused by his mother's behavior. Before I could say anything, though, he continued talking.

"I know about my mom's affair, see." The glimpse of hurt I'd seen on his face was now much more visible.

"I'm sorry, Lyle. I didn't realize she was having one."

He nodded. "She was. With Rufus." He looked up at me through hair that flopped down over his forehead and into his eyes.

I took a deep breath. "I see."

"So Mom knows I know. She thinks I went down there to tell Rufus off, blew up at him, and killed him."

I shook my head. "But you would have been at school, then."

Lyle gave me a twisted smile. "I cut school that day. Bad choice. If I'd *known* Rufus was going to be murdered, I'd have made sure I was in class. School is the perfect alibi—they know where you are every single minute of the day."

The library doors swished open and Lyle muttered. "That's my tutor. Guess I better go."

I reached out to him impulsively, putting my hand on his arm. He looked up at me in surprise and I pulled my hand back, saying, "I don't know if you're interested, but there is a great group that Luna heads up—she's our youth librarian." I stuffed a small flyer in his hand.

He gave me that smile again. "I'm not much of a reader. Which is probably why I'm always in tutoring."

"It's not just books. She hosts all kinds of activities and the group seems to get along really well." I said to Lyle, "There's even a yoga class that's about to start up soon." I added that flyer to the others I gave him.

Lyle looked like he hadn't planned on adding a yoga class to his list of things to do.

I said, "From what I can tell online, plenty of people have signed up for it. Luna's making sure it's good for beginners."

Lyle looked thoughtful for a moment. "Are there many girls there?"

I couldn't tell if that was going to be a selling point for him or not. "I think her usual group is about 95% girls, to be honest."

Lyle suddenly looked a lot more interested. "I guess it might be good for my stress."

"Yoga is awesome for stress," I agreed.

"Could you sign me up for that one, then?" he asked.

"I'll put you down for it. Just think about the book club, as well. It might be a good way to get out and meet some different people. They're all very outgoing, too."

He bobbed his head at me again and set off with his tutor.

About an hour later, Lyle had hurried out of the library again with his backpack, clearly wanting to leave math or English behind him as fast as he could. He gave me a small smile as he walked out.

To my surprise, Brownie came in shortly after her son had left. She approached Lyle's tutor before he could leave.

"Just checking in to make sure Lyle made his tutoring session," Brownie said briskly to the tutor. "He was on time?"

The tutor nodded. Before he could say anything, Brownie continued.

"And was he *engaged*?"

The tutor hesitated. "He's never going to be excited about doing extra work, but he did it."

Brownie pursed her lips as if not particularly happy with the answer. I wondered if she was still thinking of the perfect social media image of her family. Perhaps that included a son who was excessively eager to learn. Maybe she portrayed him as a true academic to her followers online.

The tutor seemed eager to get away and Brownie reluctantly let him go. She glanced over curiously at me. "I saw Lyle in the parking lot. He mentioned he'd spoken to you on the way in."

I couldn't help but put in a good word for Lyle. "He was actually here before his tutor was, so he was killing time." There was no need to mention that he'd originally wanted to just take off when he realized he'd beaten the tutor there.

"He was holding some kind of flyers or something," said Brownie.

She clearly tried to keep an eye on what he was doing all the time. Or maybe that was a new thing once she realized he'd been cutting school.

"I pointed out some of the teen activities we have here at the library," I said. "It might be a good way for him to meet some new people."

Brownie snorted. "It'll be a hard sell getting him to read a book. I have to force him to read the stuff he's assigned at school."

"We have other programs for teens. Luna, our youth librarian, spends a lot of time putting them together and always gets input from the kids. They have food-related programs, crafts, movies, and gaming nights. She's even hosted a lock-in at the library."

Brownie frowned. "What about academic-related programs?"

Brownie was just full of fun apparently. I said, "Yes, the library has also sponsored talks by local teachers on getting better scores on aptitude tests and just general testing tips."

She finally looked more interested. Then she said, "What's your opinion of Lyle?"

Now I was the one who was frowning. "My opinion of him? I don't know him well enough to be able to give one."

"I just figured you see a lot of teens with your job. Does he seem like the rest of them?"

I paused. "Well, teens are all different, of course, just like adults are. He seems like he's just trying to make his way through the teen years to me, like most kids." I added, "We do have a lot of resources for parents of teens, if you're interested. I could point you in the direction of some helpful books about healthy parent-teen relationships." I was thinking of the book I'd given Irene's aunt.

Brownie snapped, "I don't need a book to tell me how to parent my child."

I gave her a tight smile. "I just wanted to let you know the books were available if you ever need them."

But Brownie had already walked away.

Later in the afternoon, the library had settled down a little bit. I took a few minutes to skim the local paper for the first time that day.

Greta's obituary was in the paper. Although she didn't have any family in town, she was part of a large family that was rather scattered around. They were planning on holding a small memorial service later on when they could get as many family members together as possible.

I looked over at Wilson's office, saw he didn't seem to be on the phone, and walked over to tap on his door. He motioned me in.

"Hey there. How did your dinner go last night?"

Wilson looked uncertain, which was not an expression I was accustomed to seeing him wear.

"Well, she ate it. Although she did say she was very full after a small helping."

I said quickly, "Well, pot roast is pretty filling, isn't it? Lots of protein."

Wilson cheered up at this. "I guess that's true. She had a good deal of carbs, too. Mona ate a lot of dinner rolls, as I recall."

I had the feeling that didn't speak well of Wilson's dinner if Mona had filled up on bread. But I gave him a reassuring smile.

"What can I help you with?" asked Wilson.

I said, "I was thinking again about Greta after reading her obituary in the paper. It sounds to me as if the family is going to be having a private memorial service sometime later for her. But I thought the library should do something since Greta was such a loyal volunteer here."

Wilson nodded. "You're absolutely right, Ann. We most certainly should do something for her. Did the obituary give any ideas in terms of memorials or tributes?"

"It said that, in lieu of flowers, donations could be made to the Red Cross. Since she was a nurse, I think that's a nice way to remember Greta. And the organization will, of course, notify the family that the library made a donation."

"An excellent idea, Ann. Will you take care of that for us?"

"I'd be happy to."

Wilson said, "On a completely different subject—you read poetry, don't you?" His voice was brusque.

"Sure. I'm especially fond of Edna St. Vincent Millay."

He gave a dry laugh. "I don't think you'll find that these compare." He handed over a few printed pages and I glanced over them.

The poems were clearly written for Mona. But Wilson, being Wilson, they were more focused on the diction and mood and less on any romantic gestures.

Wilson was watching me intently.

"These are very nice, Wilson. I'm guessing you wrote them for Mona? I'm sure she's going to be absolutely thrilled."

And I *was* sure of that. Mona had gotten very used to the buttoned-up, serious Wilson. I was wondering what made him start changing his approach. A nice dinner? Poetry? It was quite a dramatic change for Wilson.

He said gruffly, "I'm trying to be more approachable. Warmer. I think I have a hard time with that."

"Did Mona say she wanted you to be that way?"

He shook his head. "No, but she's talked about her husband recently. He was a completely different kind of person. She said they'd eat dinner together on the sofa all cuddled up under a blanket and listen to music and just talk for hours."

From the expression on his face, it didn't look as if this scenario was something that Wilson found at all appealing.

He continued, "I found a book here at the library that was talking about 'love languages.'" He sighed. "I thought I'd give it a go."

This sounded very much like a Wilson approach. If there was something he wasn't sure about how to do, he'd research it in a book and then try and apply it.

"I'm sure she's going to love the poems," I said warmly. "And I know she really appreciated the dinner you made for her." I *was* sure of that, actually. It was the thought that counted, after all.

He looked much more cheerful. "Thanks, Ann."

I nodded and before I could say anything else, his phone rang. He always had such busy days.

Wilson gave me a rueful look. "Sorry. We'll talk later? Tomorrow, actually. After I take this, I'm going to head out early."

I nodded again and left him with his phone call.

As soon as I got behind the reference desk, I saw the doors open and Luna walk in.

I raised my eyebrows in surprise as she came over to me. "Dedication to the library? It's your day off."

Luna gave me a smile. "I wanted to talk to somebody, and you seemed like the best candidate. Plus, I know Wilson brought in the leftovers from the meal he cooked for Mom, and I wanted to make sure they disappeared so he wouldn't have his feelings hurt if he saw them in the fridge tomorrow. I think he thought the rest of the staff would help themselves, but there probably haven't been any takers."

I grimaced. "Was it that bad, then? I know he was trying to make comfort food, but the way he was planning to go about it didn't sound like it was going to work."

"I feel terrible for him because he tried so hard, but it was mostly inedible, according to my mother. Mom is a real trooper and made sure she cleaned her plate, but that was only because she'd been smart and did not put too much food on her plate to begin with."

I said, "I'll put it all in a zipper bag and take the remains home with me."

"Not to eat!" Luna looked horrified. "Don't even let Fitz take a crack at it."

"Oh, no. But I have a compost heap and it will do nicely in it, I'm sure."

Luna said, "Excellent. Good to know it can be helpful in some way."

"What I'm more interested in is hearing how your lunch with Jeremy went." I smiled at her and Luna blushed.

"Oh, I don't know. I mean—yes, it went great. Jeremy and I have a ton in common ... the same sense of humor, the same way of looking at the world. And he's a really nice guy, too. I know there's an age difference between us that makes me feel just a little self-conscious, but when we're talking with each other, it's like we're the same age."

"That's great, Luna!" And it was. As bad as I felt for Burton, it was obvious Luna was happy. She absolutely projected happiness.

A patron came up to the desk and Luna quickly said, "I should head back home. Thanks, Ann, for being an ear."

I was working on a research request from a patron when the library doors swept open and I saw Zelda and Cora coming into the building *together*. They were clearly coming in together. What was more, Zelda didn't seem to be completely vexed with Cora, despite the fact that Cora was prattling happily away.

They had tote bags with them. I asked, "Knitting club? But that was just held, wasn't it?"

Cora gave me a big smile. "It was. But a few of us from the club thought it would be fun to have a craft session that wasn't officially on the books. We just enjoy the time spent together, *making* something. When Zelda called me up and asked if I wanted to have coffee, I thought coming here would be even better."

I looked at Zelda wordlessly, not even sure which part of Cora's statement I found more surprising.

Cora asked, "Would you two excuse me for just a second? I need to run and talk to someone."

She took off and I said to Zelda, "You called Cora? And you're . . . knitting?"

I had a very hard time picturing the hard-edged, chain-smoking Zelda doing something as cozy and comforting as knitting.

Zelda shrugged. "Good stress relief. My mother showed me how to do it."

"And . . . Cora?"

Zelda sighed. "I guess I'm a softy at heart."

I strongly doubted that but waited to hear Zelda elaborate.

Zelda said in her gravelly voice, "I felt bad about Cora. You know—what she told us at Esther's funeral. Maybe I did steal Esther away from her. Maybe she did feel alone."

I nodded. "It's hard to fake loneliness." And it was clearly etched all over Cora's features.

Zelda added gruffly, "I knew she had her knitting group, but it doesn't seem like she's all that close to them—they're just knitting friends, not friend-friends. I thought I'd make an effort." She had a grim look on her face as if she believed she might sorely regret her rash actions.

"What are you knitting?" I asked.

Zelda pulled something soft and pastel out of her bag, surprising me yet again. "Thought I'd make a baby blanket. Got a great-niece who's expecting."

"That's lovely," I said, meaning it.

Cora had finished up her conversation so Zelda said, "Better go."

The two walked off over to a group of armchairs in one of the reading areas.

Chapter Seventeen

It was apparently going to be one of those afternoons where I was engaged in constant conversation. I put aside the research I was working on when Mrs. Schubert strode into the library twenty minutes after Cora and Zelda had and looked immediately over at Wilson's office. I said quickly, "I'm sorry, Mrs. Schubert. He's already left for the day. Is there anything I can help you with?"

The older lady blew out a sigh. "No, probably not. Oh, actually, maybe there is something, aside from my business with Wilson. I need something new to read."

"New as in a new release? Or just new-to-you?"

Mrs. Schubert said, "As long as I haven't read it, it'll work for me. The nonfiction book you gave me has been very helpful, of course, but I'd also like something else to entertain me."

These were sort of the open-ended book requests that drove me a little crazy, although I was very good at hiding it. "What sorts of things do you like reading?"

Mrs. Schubert waved her hand around. "All sorts of things."

"Fiction? Nonfiction?"

Mrs. Schubert glared at me as if I were being deliberately obtuse. "Fiction, of course!" she barked.

"Romance? Mystery? Literary fiction? Science fiction?"

Mrs. Schubert merely continued glaring at me, refusing to answer this question.

I took a deep breath. "I'm currently re-reading *Rebecca* by du Maurier and really enjoying it all over again. I think the library has another copy. Would you like to read it?" I realized that I'd already recommended the book to Mrs. Schubert's niece. It would be interesting if they ended up reading the same novel. Maybe they could even connect over it.

Mrs. Schubert said, "If it's what you recommend, I'll try it. That name is familiar. I might have read her books long ago."

"Are you the type of reader who can remember every character and plot, years later?" I asked.

Mrs. Schubert gave a barking laugh. "Certainly not. I have trouble even remembering where I've put my grocery list."

I said, "I'm not that sort of reader either, actually. Which is why I'm now considering a major du Maurier marathon after finishing *Rebecca*. I believe I'll pick up *My Cousin Rachel* next."

Mrs. Schubert frowned. "That title does sound familiar. Good to know there's a series."

"Oh no, she didn't write in series."

This news did not appear to please the older woman. "I do like reading series. You only have to learn the characters one time."

"I can come up with a series for you to read, if you prefer."

Mrs. Schubert waved her ringed hand dismissively. "No, I'll just take what you've suggested. I don't have much time today. I'm to help out with a flower arrangement at the church."

I had her wait at the desk while I ran off to fetch it. Thankfully, it was still in the stacks. I checked out the book to her account.

Mrs. Schubert, perhaps because my questions had annoyed her, started thinking about her niece, another young person who also annoyed her.

"Have you seen Irene recently?" she asked me.

I smiled at her. "I saw her just yesterday. I was picking up a toy for Fitz and she was working at the time. She seemed happy."

Mrs. Schubert gave a stiff nod. "Yes, that's how she appears to me, too. At least, she seems *happier*. Will wonders never cease? I hope she accepts the fact that a job can give her a sense of purpose and some security. It doesn't have to make her rich to be a good fit." She added slowly, "She also seems to have a young man now."

"Does she?" I thought back to our brief encounter with Freddie while Irene and I were standing outside the pet shop. That must have been quick.

"That's right. At least, that's what she told me on the phone this morning. I suppose he might be another fly-by-night type like the one she saw in college that wrecked everything. It's Freddie Jenkins, of all people."

I said, "Esther's son, yes."

Mrs. Shubert continued, "I understand he's inheriting Esther's considerable fortune." Her tone indicated she wasn't too pleased at that fact. "I'm sure he'll see fit to blow right through it all. He's always seemed like a big spender to me." She sniffed. "Just the same, he's been careful to woo Irene with some nice romantic gestures. I mean, it *just* started, but she's so optimistic. When she left work yesterday, he was waiting for her to get off."

"Was he?"

She nodded. "Irene was so excited that she called me up. You know, she hasn't dated since that disastrous experience in college. So when Freddie offered to take her for a nice dinner and showed up with flowers and candy, she was simply thrilled."

"That's good to hear," I said. "I know she's had a tough time."

"*I've* had a tough time," said Mrs. Schubert. "I do hope Irene is turning a new leaf and will be a lot easier to manage now." She hesitated. "There was one thing, though, that gives me pause. Esther and I used to talk occasionally. Not often, of course. She and I didn't have much in common."

I could imagine they didn't. Esther was content with her very quiet life outdoors. Mrs. Schubert was something of a society matron. If Whitby, North Carolina, had such a thing.

"One thing we *did* have in common, though, was the fact that we had younger people who were asking for handouts a lot. Esther apparently was sitting pretty, financially-speaking, although you'd never guess it. I suppose money wasn't very important to her. Anyway, we commiserated with each other. It gets old, having dependents ask you for money. Irene is constantly looking for supplemental income and it sounded like Freddie was the same way."

Mrs. Schubert was looking at me as if she expected me to say something. I quickly said, "It's very generous of you to help out. And I'm sure Freddie appreciated the assistance from his mother, too."

"Did he?" asked Mrs. Schubert doubtfully. "That's where I wonder if you're wrong, Ann. Esther was telling me that the two of them had a terrible argument just shortly before her demise. I've reported this to the police, of course, as soon as I heard Esther's death might have been foul play."

"Did Esther say what the argument was about?"

Mrs. Schubert tightened her lips into a thin line at the memory. "She certainly did. She said that Freddie was asking her for what she thought was an exorbitant amount of money. It made her wonder if maybe he weren't gambling or something. At any rate, she turned him down. Esther and I had recently been saying that it might be a kindness for both of us to allow our dependents to fend for themselves a bit more. After all, they're both adults. Maybe my niece and her son would become better, happier people if they just became more self-reliant. Anyway, I couldn't help but wonder if Freddie became so angry at being turned down that he turned on his mother. Do you know much about him?"

I shook my head. "I'm afraid I don't. I've only talked to him a couple of times."

Mrs. Schubert sighed. "And now he's dating my Irene. I can't help but wonder what my sainted sister would think about all this. I do hope he's not some hooligan who's going to make Irene's life worse than it already is. To me, it's just another indication of Irene's poor judgement. The sad thing is, as I mentioned, she's so very excited about seeing him."

I said in a comforting tone, "Maybe it will all work out. He certainly sounds eager to be having a relationship with Irene."

"I do hope you're right, Ann, and it's not going to be yet another example of Irene's bad decision-making. Well, I should be off. Please let Wilson know that I'd like to speak with him tomorrow."

She started heading toward the door but stopped still when she saw Irene coming in. Irene stopped short, too, at the sight of her aunt.

"Mercy!" said Mrs. Schubert. "Irene, what on earth are you doing here?"

"Just picking up a book Ann recommended," said Irene, sounding a bit defensive.

Mrs. Schubert blinked at her. "You read?"

Irene now looked even more defensive than she had previously. She also noticed the book her aunt was clutching and glanced over at me slightly accusingly.

I shrugged. "It's a good book. We do have another copy of it since it was a book club selection here a few years ago."

Mrs. Schubert looked even more amazed. "We're going to be reading the same book?"

The idea seemed to disagree with Irene.

Mrs. Schubert, however, seemed intrigued. "Well, then. That's very fun, isn't it, Irene? Perhaps you and I can discuss the book. Maybe over coffees?"

Irene summoned up a pleased expression. "That would be great, Aunt Mary."

Mrs. Schubert nodded to herself as if the plan was now formal. "Yes. That's what we'll do." She strode out, book in hand.

Irene gave me a wry look. "I guess it's better than our usual conversations. Those don't even qualify as conversations—it's just usually me asking for money and my aunt yelling at me."

I smiled at her. "I'll go grab the book for you."

"Thanks."

When I came back in, Irene was loving on Fitz, who had his eyes closed happily.

I checked out the book for Irene as she rubbed Fitz under his chin. She said, "You know, my aunt was so surprised with me reading that she didn't even ask me why I wasn't working."

I must have looked concerned that she'd lost the pet shop job because she laughed. "It's okay—it's just my day off. I didn't get fired . . . yet."

I smiled at her. "Glad you've got a day off. Your aunt was telling me before you came in that Freddie Jenkins asked you out."

Irene grinned at me. "Isn't that great? I haven't had a date in forever. Yeah, he was waiting outside the shop when it closed—flowers and candy in hand. Took me out for dinner and everything."

"That's great, Irene," I said. "I was thinking there was a spark between you when I saw the two of you together outside the shop."

Irene nodded. "Yeah. It's funny—the two of us have both lived here our whole lives but we never ran into each other much. Maybe we had to be at just the right time of our lives to make a connection." Then she shrugged. "And that's enough philosophizing for me today. Anyway, I was glad to have something good happening for once. The cops called me *again* just a little while ago. Said they had some information that I was spotted near the alley where Rufus was killed."

"Really?" I asked. Linus must have called Burton very shortly after our conversation.

"Yeah. I knew it was going to look bad—that's why I didn't say anything about it to begin with. I was walking by there and saw something on the ground. I feel stupid now, but I was curious so I got closer to see what it was. It was Rufus." She quickly added, "I could see he was dead, of course. There wasn't anything I could do, so I just left as fast as I could. I knew if the cops realized I was in the area, they were going to try to pin every-thing on me. And I didn't have anything to do with it."

I nodded although it pained me to hear her say Rufus had been dead because he wasn't. Maybe she could have done some-thing that would have saved him. Probably not—like Burton had said, there was nothing I could have done. But it still both-ered me.

Irene sighed. "I found out from the cops, though, that he ac-tually *wasn't* dead. That makes me feel bad. At first, I was wor-ried the cops were going to charge me with something for not calling it in . . . I don't know what they could have charged me with, but I bet they'd have been creative and figured something out. But I guess they're more worried about catching whoever did it than worrying about me."

"That's good," I said in a half-hearted way.

Irene said, "Well, I better get out of here before my aunt finds another excuse to come back in the library. See you later, Ann." She grabbed the book and headed out of the building.

The rest of the afternoon continued at a steady pace until an hour before closing where it appeared no one was in the library at all. That was so unusual that I did a careful walkabout to make sure nobody had drowsed off in the quiet section. But no one was there.

I waited until our nine o'clock closing time just the same, in case a frantic student needed to rush in and grab a resource or make a copy on our copy machine. But it was quiet.

I coaxed Fitz into his carrier, and he sleepily ambled in. I was about to walk out and lock up when I remembered the remains of Wilson's ill-fated dinner that I'd promised Luna I'd discreetly get rid of. I set the carrier carefully down and headed to the breakroom, returning with the meal in a plastic bag. Then I picked up Fitz's carrier with my free hand and headed outside.

I was locking up when I heard a voice behind me.

A chill went up my spine. I didn't have to turn around to know who it was. Brownie.

"Sorry, I'm just closing up. We'll open back up tomorrow at eight," I said in a carefully steady voice.

Brownie hissed, "I don't care about visiting the library. I care about what you and Lyle were talking about earlier."

I turned slowly around, setting Fitz's carrier down. Fitz apparently cared for Brownie's tone as little as I did because he was growling very low in his throat.

I said, "Brownie, we went over this earlier. Lyle and I were killing time before his tutor showed up. It sounded like he's had a lot on his mind lately and I handed him some flyers about the offerings for teens that we host at the library. I thought it might be a good way for him to meet some other kids he might not know from school."

Brownie's voice was icy. "Don't try to give me that."

I frowned. "You saw the flyers, Brownie."

"That wasn't the *only* thing you were talking about. Do you think I'm an idiot? I asked Lyle directly as soon as we were both back home."

Suddenly, it was all very clear to me. Brownie had killed Esther and Rufus, too.

"It's because of your affair with Rufus," I said slowly.

"See? You know more than you think you do," said Brownie with a short laugh. She casually reached in her pocket and pulled out a small pistol. It looked like a toy, but I knew it wasn't nearly as innocuous as it seemed. I took an involuntary step back.

"You stay right there," said Brownie sharply.

I said in a gasping voice, "So you're just going to shoot me right out here in the parking lot, Brownie? Don't you think somebody is going to hear that? This is right next to a residential area."

"By the time anyone does anything about it, I'll be long gone," said Brownie confidently.

Fitz's growling became more pronounced.

Stalling for time seemed to be my best tactic. At least I could put this off. I wasn't sure how good of a shot Brownie was, but it didn't seem to matter considering how close she was to me.

I cleared my throat. "Esther was your original target for a reason, wasn't she? She'd spend her days practically as part of the background. But that meant she always had a finger on the pulse of the town. She took everything in. And one day, she took in the fact that you and Rufus seemed extremely close."

"She was a nosy old woman who got what was coming to her," said Brownie with a snarl.

My mouth was so dry that I had a tough time speaking. "Esther might not even have seen you with Rufus at the square. She probably saw you when he came by the house, didn't she? That makes the most sense. Your husband is often away on business trips and your son is in school—most of the time. Is that how

Lyle found out about your affair? Did he cut school one time and find Rufus over at your house?"

Her eyes flashed. "Lyle had no business cutting school to begin with."

"No. But you were able to exert some control over Lyle. Besides, he was probably just as invested as you were in keeping the family intact. On the other hand, you had absolutely no control over Esther. You were worried she was going to tell someone and then your husband would leave you. That wouldn't work for you—you're a social media influencer and you've created this image of a perfect home and family."

Brownie gave me a crooked smile and gestured at me with the pistol. "Go ahead. I want to hear where you're going with this."

I swallowed, but it was a dry swallow. "I'm thinking you probably wanted to eliminate Esther very privately. Since you were neighbors, you'd have rather slipped over there when no one was at your house or visiting her. The thing with Esther, though, is that she spent so much time away from her house. When she was home, there would also have been people around you at your house."

Brownie quirked an eyebrow and I added, "Or maybe you just acted rashly. You'd left the coffeehouse, which is very close to the square, and Esther called out to you. She mentioned something about you and Rufus. You were angry and couldn't seem to reason with her. Maybe you even offered her money to 'unsee' what she'd noticed. The only problem with that was that Esther had plenty of money, herself. She wasn't motivated by it. Maybe you never really meant to kill her. Maybe you were just frustrated and you gave her a quick shove. When you saw what had happened, you were shocked."

Brownie drawled, "Well, I do believe you've hit on it. You must feel awfully smart."

I took a deep breath, wishing someone would drive by or walk through the parking lot as they took their dog out. But it was totally silent out there, aside from Fitz's low-key growling. "The only problem was Greta. She saw what happened . . . or so you thought. She'd been going around town fussing about Esther being pushed. She wasn't totally *sure* what else she'd seen. Here's where it gets a little tricky."

"I'm all ears," said Brownie dryly.

"You thought Greta knew you'd killed Esther. But instead, she was talking about a different incident—when Rufus was acting rough with her. Rufus knew you were worried about having your affair made public and he threatened Esther on your behalf. Greta witnessed that because she told a neighbor that it had been Rufus she's seen. But you thought she'd seen *you*."

Brownie looked surprised at the information that Greta hadn't witnessed her murdering Esther. Then she gave that twisted smile again. "Go on."

"You couldn't allow Greta to start thinking more about what she'd seen, though. Once she heard that Esther was dead, she was going to put two and two together and figure out what she'd seen. So you paid a visit on her one day to ensure that didn't happen. It was another shove—this time a more calculated one." I paused, looking at Brownie's dead expression. Then I said, "But then there was Rufus."

I saw a flicker of emotion cross her features at his name. I said, "You and Rufus were having an affair. I'm guessing it wasn't a big deal for you because you weren't exactly looking for a love match. But Rufus—he took it more seriously. Once everything suddenly got complicated after you'd committed two murders, you were ready to break things off with Rufus. After all, you needed to work hard to maintain that image of your perfect life that you'd created online."

"It *is* a perfect life," Brownie interjected. "It's not that it just *seems* that way."

I disagreed, but with a gun pointing at me, wasn't really in a position to argue. "You told Rufus you wanted to break things off. Rufus, on the other hand, didn't want to. Maybe he thought things were more serious between the two of you. You could have allowed him to believe that they were. He was shocked and maybe angry. He could have felt taken advantage of. At any rate, he was probably acting less than discreet. You couldn't allow him to let people know about the affair. What if gossip reached your husband's ears? At that point, you'd already killed two people and a third would have been pretty easy. You were out early, waited until the shop was quiet and Rufus was in the alley, then hit him over the head while he was putting things in the dumpster."

"It wasn't very helpful when you attempted to resuscitate him," said Brownie snidely.

I felt a little jab of pain at the memory of how useless I'd felt after my efforts were unrewarded. That might have been why the next thing I said came out so harshly. "You were facing more problems than just Rufus nearly surviving his attack. Lyle knew about the affair. Your solution to that problem was to throw him under the bus and have *him* take responsibility for the murders if law enforcement came too close to figuring out the real solution."

Brownie glowered at me. "He wouldn't even really get into any trouble, you know, because of his age. He would get juvenile detention or something like that."

"Then you'd be able to say he was off at boarding school or something and would continue with your sham of a perfect life online."

Brownie tilted her head to one side thoughtfully. "You're actually pretty smart. I had the feeling you might be. That's why I was worried when Lyle told me he'd been talking to you. Not that being smart is going to do you any good."

She steadied the gun. Which was when I slammed the bag with the glass Pyrex dish and Wilson's disgusting meal as hard as I could into her arm.

Chapter Eighteen

Brownie wasn't expecting it—a librarian who fights back. The gun went flying off into the darkness of the library parking lot and she gave a howl of pain from the glass dish's impact on her arm. Maybe I'd broken it. At this point, I wasn't waiting to find out. I grabbed Fitz's carrier, pulled my keys out of my pocket, and got into my car as fast as I could.

I started up the motor with a roar and looked in my rearview mirror. I saw that Brownie was gone.

I picked up my phone and called Burton. "The murderer is Brownie. She just pointed a gun at me when I was locking up at the library. I hit her with something and she took off."

"Got it," said Burton in a grim voice. "She's not going to get far. Don't go home, okay? Just in case she knows where you live."

So I headed over to Grayson's house. He opened the door, looking bleary-eyed as if he'd just woken up. "Ann? What happened?"

I took a deep breath and then felt tears prickle in my eyes. I blinked them back and said, "I found out who the killer was."

His eyes grew huge as I told him the story. He had me sit on the sofa and got me a drink. He said, "Brownie. Wow. And she was planning on Lyle taking the blame for it. What kind of mom does that?"

"She's definitely not in the running for Mom of the Year," I agreed dryly.

"I hope Burton is able to catch up with her."

I nodded. "She's got to be pretty desperate at this point. But, thinking about it, where could she hide in Whitby? It's a small town and once Burton says she's wanted in relation to several murders, everyone is going to keep an eye out for her."

"Was she in a car?"

I shook my head. "She was on foot, but there must have been a car nearby somewhere. She probably just didn't want to park there in case someone drove by and saw it." I shivered a little, thinking about the precautions Brownie had built into her plan to kill me.

Grayson saw the shiver and instantly brought me a blanket from his linen closet.

I said in a wry voice, "Shouldn't I be the one taking care of you?"

He shook his head. "Not anymore. I woke up from a nap this afternoon feeling completely well. I've just been taking it easy the rest of the time—I'd even taken another short nap right before you came here."

Grayson set about distracting me from the events of the evening. He turned on the TV and loaded some goofy movie that he'd enjoyed when he was in college. It was the kind of mindless fare that I never sought out on my own but found very distracting under the circumstances.

It was a long while before I got a phone call from Burton.

"We got her," he said with grim satisfaction. "Are you okay?"

"I'm here at Grayson's house." I gave him the address when he asked for it.

"I'm heading over," he said.

Burton arrived just minutes later, and the kind look in his eyes was enough to make those tears prickle again. I took a deep breath and settled myself down.

"I'm sorry this had to happen to you," he said. "Can you tell me what happened?"

I nodded. "Brownie thought I was one step ahead from where I was in terms of putting the pieces together. If I'd really known what was going on, I'd have called you, Burton. In fact, there was some information I'd gotten that afternoon that I was planning on passing along. I'd talked with Lyle at the library while he was waiting for his tutor to show up. He said he thought Brownie believed he was the one who was the murderer."

Burton said slowly, "Okay. But clearly, she didn't believe that since she was the one who was responsible."

"Exactly. Apparently, she was setting up Lyle to take the blame for the murders, though. She said something about him just getting juvenile detention because of his age."

Burton shook his head, looking sad.

"But the big thing I gleaned from my conversation with Lyle and what I'd especially wanted to pass along to you was that Lyle knew his mother had been having an affair with Rufus."

Burton's eyes opened wide. "That changes everything."

"Right. And I think that's what got Brownie so worried—worried enough to try to get rid of me. If Rufus and Brownie were having an affair, it put everything in a different context. It meant Esther might have seen something Brownie didn't want her to see. That Greta had seen Brownie shove Esther. That Rufus had to go because he either threatened to expose their affair publicly or didn't want the affair to end at all."

"And Brownie has set up this whole, perfect-looking world online. That's her job, actually. She's selling her lifestyle and gets kickbacks from clothing companies and other places," said Burton.

I nodded. "It's all a façade, though. The truth is that Brownie's whole life was teetering on the edge, about to self-destruct. Her son is having academic issues and apparently is resistant to being part of his mother's influencer world. Her husband, Blaze, is absent a lot—traveling for work, supposedly. And Brownie, far from being the perfect wife she's portraying herself as, was having an affair with another man."

"So she gets rid of everyone who has the power to make that little fantasy world explode. Even, apparently, to the extent of letting her son take the blame for everything. I wonder how she'd have explained juvenile detention to her loyal followers?"

I shrugged. "I figured she'd just explain that he was off at boarding school or something. That wouldn't have seemed out of the ordinary to her followers, probably."

Grayson said grimly, "Quick thinking with the bag of leftovers, Ann."

I gave a humorless laugh. "Well, necessity is the mother of invention. Or maybe desperation is. At any rate, I didn't have a whole lot of choices. It's good Wilson's meal was useful for something."

Burton chuckled. "Am I to understand that Wilson isn't much of a cook?"

I smiled at him. "So far, he hasn't shown himself to be. But he did pick a tough meal to cook quickly. Poor Mona. Anyway, the remains ended up in our breakroom fridge and I promised Luna I'd take them home and dispose of them."

"I'd say you disposed of them," drawled Burton. "From what I saw in the library parking lot, the force of the hit made them sprawl all over the asphalt." He paused and then said carefully, "I guess you know about Luna and me, Ann."

I nodded. "I was sorry to hear about it."

Burton took a deep breath and let it out slowly. "Yeah. I was too, but part of me realized it was coming. Not necessarily that Luna would be interested in seeing someone else, but that things were coming to a close. She's right—we are very different people. Sometimes opposites attract and sometimes it's just too wide of a gulf."

Grayson said quietly, "I hope you find someone else soon, Burton."

He brightened. "Maybe I will. And it wasn't like my time with Luna was wasted time—I enjoyed every minute." He stood up. "Now I need to leave you two and head back over to the station. I'm relieved this one is wrapped up. The fact there were three deaths shows how desperate and reckless Brownie was getting."

"There were almost four deaths," said Grayson, looking grim.

"Ann's quick-thinking saved the day. See you two soon."

As soon as Burton left, Grayson said, "Are you sure you're all right, Ann?"

"Never better. It feels good to know that Brownie is going behind bars. Thank goodness she never got very far on making her library board inquiries. I feel bad for Lyle, though. He didn't deserve any of this."

Grayson said, "Maybe this is going to end up working out better for him than we think. It sounds like his relationship with his mom was pretty toxic, especially since she was planning on letting him take the fall for something she did. Maybe he'll end up getting closer to his dad."

I nodded. "It'll mean his dad will have to figure out how to spend more time in town. But you're right—it could end up working out better for Lyle."

Grayson thought for a minute. "This is a pretty big story for the paper. Would you be at all interested in being interviewed?" He quickly added, "I don't want to ruin your privacy or anything."

I chuckled at that. "There's no privacy in a small town. Word is probably already starting to go around, despite the hour. Sometimes it's good to control the narrative. And have it be the actual truth."

Grayson brightened. "Great! But let's do this down at the newspaper office tomorrow morning so we don't blur the lines here."

I said, "Why don't we head over to your office now? Is there enough time to change the front page of the paper for tomorrow's edition?"

Grayson looked at his watch. "I think so. It would mean having the paper come out a little later tomorrow morning.

Are you sure you're up to doing an interview tonight, though? You've been through a lot, Ann."

"I'm up to it—I don't see myself sleeping at all tonight after all that. But are you? You're the one who's been sick in bed for days."

Grayson smiled at me. "Let's do it. And we can introduce Fitz to my office. But first, I'm going to order take-out for both of us. We can pick it up along the way."

Just thirty minutes later, Fitz was happily exploring the nooks and crannies of the newspaper office and I was running through the events of the evening while eating shrimp and grits from Quittin' Time.

The door to the newspaper office opened and Abby stood there. She looked a little taken aback at the scene in front of her—the fact that I was there, the orange and white cat who came bounding over to greet her, and the dinner Grayson and I were sharing.

"Hey," she said, only looking at Grayson. "I saw your car here and the lights on. Did you need any help?"

He looked up absently from his computer. "Hmm? Oh. No thanks, Abby. I've got everything I need."

And, as Abby stalked out, I reflected that Grayson really did have a way with words.

About the Author

Elizabeth writes the Southern Quilting mysteries and Memphis Barbeque mysteries for Penguin Random House and the Myrtle Clover series for Midnight Ink and independently. She blogs at ElizabethSpannCraig.com/blog, named by Writer's Digest as one of the 101 Best Websites for Writers. Elizabeth makes her home in Matthews, North Carolina, with her husband. She's the mother of two.

Sign up for Elizabeth's free newsletter to stay updated on releases:

https://bit.ly/2xZUXqO

This and That

I love hearing from my readers. You can find me on Facebook as Elizabeth Spann Craig Author, on Twitter as elizabethscraig, on my website at elizabethspanncraig.com, and by email at elizabethspanncraig@gmail.com.

Thanks so much for reading my book...I appreciate it. If you enjoyed the story, would you please leave a short review on the site where you purchased it? Just a few words would be great. Not only do I feel encouraged reading them, but they also help other readers discover my books. Thank you!

Did you know my books are available in print and ebook formats? Most of the Myrtle Clover series is available in audio and some of the Southern Quilting mysteries are. Find the audiobooks here: https://elizabethspanncraig.com/audio/

Please follow me on BookBub for my reading recommendations and release notifications.

I'd also like to thank some folks who helped me put this book together. Thanks to my cover designer, Karri Klawiter, for her awesome covers. Thanks to my editor, Judy Beatty for her help. Thanks to beta readers Amanda Arrieta, Rebecca Wahr, Cassie Kelley, and Dan Harris for all of their helpful suggestions and careful reading. Thanks to my ARC readers for helping to spread the word. Thanks, as always, to my family and readers.

Other Works by Elizabeth

Myrtle Clover Series in Order (be sure to look for the Myrtle series in audio, ebook, and print):

Pretty is as Pretty Dies

Progressive Dinner Deadly

A Dyeing Shame

A Body in the Backyard

Death at a Drop-In

A Body at Book Club

Death Pays a Visit

A Body at Bunco

Murder on Opening Night

Cruising for Murder

Cooking is Murder

A Body in the Trunk

Cleaning is Murder

Edit to Death

Hushed Up

A Body in the Attic

Murder on the Ballot

Death of a Suitor

A Dash of Murder

Death at a Diner (late 2022)

Southern Quilting Mysteries in Order:

Quilt or Innocence

Knot What it Seams

Quilt Trip

Shear Trouble
Tying the Knot
Patch of Trouble
Fall to Pieces
Rest in Pieces
On Pins and Needles
Fit to be Tied
Embroidering the Truth
Knot a Clue
Quilt-Ridden
Needled to Death
A Notion to Murder
Crosspatch (late 2022)

The Village Library Mysteries in Order (Debuting 2019):

Checked Out
Overdue
Borrowed Time
Hush-Hush
Where There's a Will
Frictional Characters
Spine Tingling

Memphis Barbeque Mysteries in Order (Written as Riley Adams):

Delicious and Suspicious
Finger Lickin' Dead
Hickory Smoked Homicide
Rubbed Out

And a standalone "cozy zombie" novel: Race to Refuge, written as Liz Craig

9 781955 395083